Holiday Crown

Nikki Jefford

No part of this book may be reproduced, distributed, or transmitted in any form or by any means, or stored in a database retrieval system, without the prior written permission of the author. Thank you for respecting the rights of the author.

This is a work of fiction. Any resemblance of characters to actual persons, living or dead, is purely coincidental.

Copyright © 2019 Nikki Jefford
Cover design by Najla Qamber
All rights reserved.
ISBN-13: 9781673233575

Dedicated in loving memory to my dad who looked for the humor in everything.

CHAPTER ONE

Melarue

There were so many cool things about Earth. One of my favorites . . . the toy warehouses! Seriously mind-bending. Row after row lined with shelf after shelf filled with games, action figures, stuffed animals, dolls, and baubles.

Dressed in my pair of snug blue jeans, white tank top, and the awesome pleather jacket Lyklor had gotten me for my birthday, I continued my preliminary walk-through, slowing down in the aisle lined with bicycles. A rainbow of colors unrolled down the aisle. Round rubber tires beneath bright orange, red, blue, yellow, green, and green-*and*-yellow frames. I peered closer at a wicked black bicycle with orange tire rims and handlebars. Images of bike races through the halls of Dahlquist flooded my mind. Hmm. Wouldn't that be fun?

I started humming "Deck the Halls." I wasn't sure of the lyrics, only the "fa la la la" part. That's why I preferred humming to singing—knowing the words didn't matter.

5

"Hmm hm hm, hm hm hm hm hmm. Fa la la la la, la la la la."

A teenage employee wearing a royal blue polo and black slacks paused in her stride down the aisle to smile at me. She cradled a large stuffed snowman in a Santa hat in one arm. "'Tis the season to be jolly," she said cheerfully.

How nice.

"That it is," I said, smiling back.

"Santa's little elves are busy, busy, busy this time of year."

Umm. "Sure." I forced a smile, reminding myself she was being friendly and didn't know any better. Too bad more humans weren't aware of the elven and faerie realms. They could do with a dose of cultural enlightening. Oh well. I knew how lucky I was to travel the three realms on a regular basis.

The young woman hugged Frosty to her chest and said, "Let's get you back on your shelf, why don't we?"

Resuming my stroll down the aisle, I stopped in front of a cute pink-and-white bicycle with a white-and-pink-daisy basket. Hmm, way too girly for my niece, Fraya. I wondered if they had a larger one for Aerith.

"Make way; make way," Ryo called at the end of the aisle, even though no one stood in his path. A red baseball cap with a white pom-pom on top covered his black head of hair. He wore jeans and a snug long-sleeve black tee.

Lyklor rounded the corner with a large cart, barreling toward me. Ryo jogged beside him, egging him on. "Onward,

Dasher!" My mates reached me in no time. Their grins reminded me of our boys—playful, sweet, and mischievous.

Stopping inches from my legs, Lyklor removed a hand from the cart to sweep back his messy blond hair. If he wanted, he could have been a male model in the human realm. Instead, he posed for me every day. Yep, life was pretty much sweetberry sunshine for this redheaded elf.

"Let's see what you boys found." I leaned over the cart, looking at the assortment of plastic guns and refill packs.

Ryo pointed inside, announcing, "Longstrike Nerf Modulus Toy Blaster with barrel extension, bipod, scopes, and six dart clips."

"And that there is the Nerf Rival Nemesis, fully motorized with foam bullets," Lyklor said.

"We found tactical vests with multiple dart clips." Ryo pulled one out and put it on over his tee.

"Refills to last a year at least," Lyklor added.

After taking inventory of the supplies I'd wanted, I lifted my head and grinned. "Excellent. Now that we have our gifts, what should we get the boys for Christmas?" Lyklor snorted. Ignoring him, I swept my arm down the aisle. "I was thinking bicycles."

Ryo rubbed his chin as he eyed the spoked tires lining the floor. "Do you think they would draw too much attention in Pinemist?"

I sighed moodily, my eyes lifting to the tall, overhead warehouse ceiling. I understood why Ryo asked. Elves weren't keen on "polluting" their culture with outside influences. Fae weren't any better. They wanted to keep their realms pure of man-made creations and customs—including Christmas. We celebrated winter solstice, not Santa. It was one of the reasons Hensley had asked us to rule Dahlquist during the holidays. She wanted to spend Thanksgiving, Christmas, and New Year's with her mother in Seattle.

My brood and I had spent enough time in the mortal realm to adopt some new traditions. Christmas was one of our favorites, and we didn't care if it wasn't celebrated in the elven realm or Faerie. We were rulers and rule breakers.

As Lyklor joined Ryo in pursing his lips, looking over the bikes, I was reminded of the commotion we'd caused with our large outdoor trampoline. Elves passing by had gawked as though a spaceship had landed in the field beside our cottage. That didn't stop their kids from sneaking over to bounce with our boys. Fraya had all but begged Jhaeros to get one for his estate grounds, but my brother-in-law had said if she wanted to jump up and down like a rabbit, she could go over to the cottage and do so with her cousins. Yep, that was me, the eccentric auntie. I definitely had to find her a bicycle.

"I was thinking for the castle," I said.

My mates stared at one another, thinking it over much too long.

"That could be a disaster," Lyklor said.

Ryo nodded. "We should totally do it."

Triumph lifted my chin. "Two against one. Fa la la, ha-ha."

"Very well," Lyklor said. "But we'll need helmets and probably knee and arm pads, too."

"Don't forget the bells and horns," I said. "We need one for each bike."

"And how many bicycles are we talking?" Lyklor raised a brow.

"The boys, Fraya, us, Aerith, Jhaeros, Gayla, and Folas, so . . ." I did some quick counting on my fingers before looking at Lyklor with a grin. "Eleven."

We'd dragged Folas and his daughter, Gayla, into our new tradition. Gayla was a darling little girl of eight years. Unfortunately, things hadn't worked out well between Folas and his mate. The female had left him and their daughter after Gayla's third year. Father and daughter made Dahlquist their full-time home, and as far as I was concerned, they were an extended part of our family.

Lyklor rubbed the back of his neck above his favorite red leather jacket. "We're going to need help teleporting all this back to Dahlquist."

Ryo nodded, the white pom-pom bobbing on top of his baseball cap. "Maybe we should finish filling the cart with the smaller stuff."

"Follow me." Lyklor turned the cart around and wheeled it down the aisle at a rapid pace.

I practically had to jog to keep up with my golden-haired mate. He led us to an aisle filled with dolls and stuffed animals. There was way too much pink and purple going on.

Pushing the cart aside, Lyklor grabbed a boxed doll, while Ryo picked up a pink fluffy kitten.

"I think Gayla would really like this human doll with her rounded ears," Lyklor said.

"And I know she would love this cat. She's always excited to visit the animals in the stable," Ryo said, petting the stuffed toy.

"Get both," I suggested.

Lyklor and Ryo looked at one another and shrugged before tossing both toys into the cart. I was ready to move on to more exciting playthings, but Lyklor pushed the cart down the girls' aisle at a snail's pace while scanning each shelf.

"Aw," Ryo cooed.

"What?" Lyklor asked, stopping the cart.

Ryo swiped a pink headband dangling from a peg and held it up for inspection. "Look. It has cute little cat ears. We should get this to go with Gayla's kitten."

"She can be big sister cat," Lyklor said.

Ryo nodded.

Silly boys.

"Look at this," Lyklor said, snatching a box from the shelf. "Lip balm boutique." He turned the box around, squinting to read the back. "You can create custom flavors. There's beeswax, molds, containers, and an instruction pamphlet. Gayla's taken an interest in powders and potions. This is perfect!"

"Not to mention safer," Ryo said under his breath.

No sooner had Lyklor placed the lip balm kit into the cart than he grabbed another boxed toy. "Polly Pocket snow globe set. Look, there's a cute little chairlift for the little Polly doll to ride up the mountain—and a snowboard to ride down."

Shaking my head, I pushed my long red hair over my shoulders. "Well, I'm glad girls' toys excite the two of you so much."

Lyklor returned the toy to its place on the shelf, cleared his throat, and glanced at Ryo. My dark-haired mate rubbed his chin and lifted both eyebrows at Lyklor. Something was up.

"Guys, what is it?"

Ryo pulled his Christmas cap off before nodding at Lyklor. They seemed to be having a silent conversation, one I really wanted in on soon.

Clasping his hands together, Lyklor stepped around the cart to stand a couple feet in front of me. "Okay, here it is, Melarue. Ryo and I would like a daughter, and we're hoping you might, too."

My jaw slackened as a soft buzz went through my belly. "You want another baby?"

"A girl," Lyklor said.

A whole new kind of giddy came over me that no amount of toy shopping could supplant. My legs twitched with the urge to skip around the store. I loved being a mom. I never would have believed it as a young teenage elf, but there was nothing quite as badass as giving birth. I'd thought shuffling around with a bulging belly would have had me groaning in frustration, but growing a life had been the most incredible, out-of-worlds experience. It had been eight years since I'd given birth to the twins. Getting pregnant had so much appeal that I wouldn't need much convincing, nor did I care about the gender, but my mates didn't need to know that. I should make them work for it a little longer.

I folded my arms. "Let's say I'm on board with this baby thing. You can't just pick out the gender like a boxed doll."

"Gender fertility spell," Lyklor blurted, his eyes shining in eager anticipation. "They're not guaranteed, but they've been known to have a highly successful rate."

"Uh-huh. And who would be doing the honors?"

Lyklor's pupils dilated as they locked onto me. "I called dibs."

"Dibs?" I scoffed. "I'm not a slice of sweetberry pie."

Ryo snorted. "Real smooth, pit head."

Sending a quick glare Ryo's way, Lyklor returned his attention to me. "You had Ryo's babies last. Plus, he got two."

I looked over at Ryo, who sighed deeply. "You have my consent. We were actually hoping for results by Christmas so we can announce it to the boys after opening gifts. You know, save the best gift for last." Ryo flashed me the cutest, most kissable smile. Then again, the thought of my golden-haired king knocking me up again made me suddenly eager to leave Ryo to handle the toy situation while Lyklor and I grabbed some alone time at the hotel. Thanksgiving was a week and a half away, and Hensley wanted us back at the castle to take over for her and Liri. We'd just have to try for baby number four at Dahlquist. That was where all my kids had been conceived. Just once it would have been cool to create life in the mortal or elven realm. At least I had a good track record for getting pregnant in Faerie.

A wide smile spread over Lyklor's cheeks. "Sarfina's been helping me look into gender spell rituals."

Ryo rolled his eyes. "Of course she has."

"Wait. Hold up." I held up my palm. "You discussed this with your sister . . . before me?"

Ryo smirked as I glowered at Lyklor.

The blond king blanched. "Uhhh . . . only because I wanted to know if it was possible before I got your hopes up."

"You mean *your* hopes." I laughed at his unease. "Whatever. The holidays must be going to my head, because I'm going to let this one fly. However, Sarfina has to stay at Ravensburg with Teryani while we try. I won't tolerate her hounding us for progress reports every hour."

"Done," Lyklor said.

"Can I hound the two of you every hour?" Ryo asked with a smirk.

"Don't you dare," Lyklor warned him.

Ryo sauntered over, his shoulder brushing mine as he took a place beside me. "Don't worry, Mel. If golden boy fails to impregnate you, I get my turn to try next holiday season."

"It won't come to that." Lyklor lifted his nose with confidence.

"We'll see," Ryo answered.

I was only half listening now. Thanks to my guys, I'd been officially bitten by the baby bug. I could already picture us announcing the news, not only to the boys, but to my sister, Jhaeros, Fraya, Folas, and Gayla as we gathered around the Christmas tree. We'd do a "hot cocoa with marshmallows" toast.

Yeah, when I put my mind to something, there was no stopping me.

Lyklor had no idea what he'd volunteered for. We weren't leaving the bedroom until I was good and pregnant. The castle staff would just have to deliver our meals to our door.

Oh, what fun we were going to have this holiday at Dahlquist.

CHAPTER TWO

Melarue

Cinnamon-scented candles labeled "Christmas Spice" flamed from jars placed around the guest chamber in Jastra's corridor. According to Lyklor, the feminine energy from one of his sister's suites would help give us a girl. Sounded woo-woo to me, but that was the Fae for you. I was just ready to get this sex fest started. If we didn't have success soon, there would be no special announcement on Christmas morning.

Red rose petals covered the white bedspread of a king-sized sleigh bed. A lacy pink see-through night gown had been laid out and draped over the edge of the bed.

Yeah, right. I folded my arms and turned up my nose at the garment. Lyklor knew me better than that. And what was with the rose petals?

While waiting for my silver-tongued mate to show up, I went ahead and brushed the flower petals off the bed with the sweep of my arm. Nope, I had no interest in turning into an elven flower blossom with petals stuck all over my naked body.

There was a knock at the door. Taking a seat on the edge of the bed, I called out, "Come in."

Dressed in a long pink, silk robe, Lyklor stepped inside. I would have burst into laughter if he hadn't pulled Lulu in after him and closed the door. The purple-and-blue-haired servant wore a blindfold and noise cancelling headphones from the mortal world. Lyklor assisted her, walking the petite faerie to a spot between the wall and bed. After positioning her to face the bed, Lyklor released her shoulders and turned to me with a pleased grin, as though he'd arranged something truly marvelous.

Words stuck in my throat. Mouth frozen in shock, an explanation for Lulu's presence was offered before I could ask Lyklor whether he'd lost his mind.

"I figured if anyone knew a gender fertility song, it was Lulu here," Lyklor announced. "Turns out she knows several." He puffed up his chest and grinned as though expecting my praise at this bit of foresight.

Once I regained control of my vocal cords, I demanded, "What the freak berries? You expect me to make a baby in here with Lulu standing at the end of the bed?"

Lyklor's smile vanished. "She can't see or hear us. All I have to do is tap her shoulder, and she'll start singing."

It wasn't enough to tell me this, naturally. Lyklor went and tapped Lulu's shoulder. The sweet Fae burst into song, a passionate melody about two dragons who created a daughter from the heat of their love.

Okay, I liked that she was singing about dragons and not baby birds as she'd once tried back at Ravensburg, but no way did I want an audience—not even someone who couldn't see or hear. She was still in the room with us.

"Lyklor, you know my rule." I had to raise my voice to be heard over Lulu. "If you want a third party in the bedroom with us, it has to be Ryo."

Sighing, Lyklor turned to Lulu and tapped her shoulder. The singing stopped. He pulled off her headphones. "Thanks, Lulu. I'll take it from here. You can go."

"Good luck, Queen Melarue." Eyes still covered; Lulu waved at an armchair near the bed.

I bit back my groan. Every time we returned to the castle, I had to retrain the staff not to call me "queen." Sure, I was married to not one king but two. I helped rule when our family was in residence. Each of my sons was a prince of Dahlquist. But I wore no crown, nor thought of myself as queen. Hensley could have that title and keep it, even when she was away. I was just Mel, married to two part-time Fae kings and mother of three . . . soon to be four once Lyklor stopped messing around.

"Alone at last," I teased my mate once he'd closed the two of us in.

He sauntered back to the bed, which might have gotten me hot with anticipation if it weren't for the pink robe.

"You're taking that off, right?" I eyed the silk dressing gown.

"Oh, it's coming off," Lyklor purred. He strutted to the spot Lulu had vacated, turning his back to me as he disrobed. The silk slid off his muscled arms and legs, rippling into a limp pile on the floor. Lyklor flexed his butt cheeks. Now this was more like it.

I licked my lips in anticipation. Lyklor turned slowly. When he faced me, my eyes bulged in their sockets. I burst into laughter a second later. Symbols had been painted in black ink all over the front of my mate's body. Circles of paint were brushed around his nipples. Attached to the circles were plus symbols. The outline of an Egyptian woman was drawn over his abdomen. At the V above his groin, a triangle had been painted pointing down with a dark line halfway up the triangle's point. More symbols covered his sides.

"Wow," I said, blinking rapidly then erupting into more laughter. I fell onto my back and clutched my stomach, rocking slightly.

As my laughter subsided and my arms relaxed, a silky voice spoke above me. "Finished?"

"Maybe. I mean, no promises." I grinned to myself then gasped when Lyklor unfastened my pants and yanked them to my ankles. I took in a trembling breath, all traces of humor winking out when I stared at Lyklor up close, naked, hard, and covered in paint.

"Take off your panties so I can give you my blessings," Lyklor said, pointing the engorged head of his shaft between my legs.

His command made me instantly wet. I did as he asked, flinging the scrap of cotton aside. I opened my legs, ready to have his needy heat join mine. Lyklor took a step toward me, then another. His hands were almost on my thighs when the door burst open and two short figures covered in white bedsheets ran in yelling, "Boo!"

"I am the ghost of Cirrus," one said.

"And I am the ghost of Albedo," said the other.

I bit my tongue to stop my scream. I didn't want to draw attention my way, though I wished I could snatch one of their sheets to cover up. Instead, I crossed my legs and wrapped my arms over my bosom. In addition to setting boundaries, we really needed to work on what constituted appropriate humor with the twins.

Lyklor's lips thinned in annoyance. Slowly, he lifted to his full height and turned to face Reed and Ronin. He placed his hands on his hips. "You ghouls know Halloween was last month, right?"

Yanking the sheets off, the twins mirrored one another, gaping at Lyklor's nether regions, screaming in horror. They turned their dark heads and ran out, leaving the sheets behind.

"That's right, and don't come back!" Lyklor hollered after them, storming to the door. He slammed it shut, bare feet pounding over the floor as he returned. He glanced over his shoulder and grumbled, "I know Ryo sent them here to disturb us."

"We can blame him for scarring the boys for life."

Lyklor huffed. "Like they haven't seen a dick before."

"Not one that's about to enter their mother."

Lyklor's irritation evaporated when he saw me still naked on the edge of the bed. Gaze hooded, his voice dropped to a husky timber. "That's right. Where were we? Oh yes, blessings and babies."

"Bay-*bee*," I enunciated. "Singular. Lyklor Elmray, I swear to Sky Mother if you knock me up with twins, there's going to be hell to pay. And while we're at it, you better give me a girl. I've come to the recent conclusion that I'm already up to my elbows in boys."

"No twins. No boys. And no more delays," Lyklor said, making good on the last part when he gripped my hips and entered me.

Eyes closed and head lifted to the ceiling, Lyklor chanted while making love. I couldn't decide whether I found it erotic or hysterical. I opted for middle ground. After finishing, Lyklor walked to a vanity mirror and looked himself over—probably to see if his paint job had smeared.

"You put that paint on yourself, right?" I called over.

"Uh, yeah, totally." Before I could ask if he was telling me the answer I wanted to hear rather than the truth, a light tapping came from the door. Lyklor's nostrils flared. "Who is it?" he called out in irritation.

HOLIDAY CROWN

"It's Peridot, Your Majesty," came the sweet voice of the female who had served as our nanny and now babysitter. Her help would come in handy for Fae baby number four. Well, elf-Fae if we were getting technical.

"What do you need?" Lyklor asked.

"I have the butterfly pollen you requested," Peridot replied.

Lyklor's eyes lit up. "Just a minute." Snatching the pink robe off the floor, Lyklor put it on as he rushed to the door and opened it a crack. "Thanks," he said briskly.

"Good luck, Mel!" Peridot called into the room before Lyklor shut the door.

I sighed. This was getting ridiculous.

Lyklor strode back to me, holding a small dark brown glass jar between his thumb and pointer fingers. He beamed with satisfaction, chest lifted, as he set the bottle on the nightstand. "Increases fertility and chances of giving birth to a girl. Let me get you a glass of water to add the butterfly pollen to. It will go down easier that way."

My mate fetched two waters, pouring from a ceramic pitcher on a small table against the wall. We emptied our glasses, along with a touch of butterfly pollen, and got back to it.

When evening came around, a tray of whole grains, lentils, and sautéed leafy greens was delivered to our door, along with lemonade. (Supposed health foods for fertility. Except for the lemonade—that was for washing it down.) After digging into the food, I took a warm, soothing bath.

My hair was piled on top of my head in a messy bun to keep it from getting soaked. *Baby or not, this is bliss,* I thought, leaning my head against the edge of the tub and closing my eyes.

"Mind if I join you?" a husky voice asked.

"Aren't you afraid to wash off the symbols?" I asked.

Lyklor glanced down at his chest. "I can paint them back on later."

"Or I could," I suggested in a sultry tone.

Lyklor's eyes glittered as his head snapped back up. He stepped into the large tub, his erection as hard as an arrowhead, and lowered himself into the water. My mate climbed over me, and soon water was sloshing over the tub's edge as we slid against one another.

"Find anything interesting about tub sex and fertility in your research?" I teased, nipping his pointed ear.

Groaning, Lyklor rocked faster.

Once clean and relaxed, I traipsed into the candlelit bedchamber and collapsed onto the bed. A nap was starting to sound mighty fine. My eyes drifted closed while Lyklor finished rinsing and drying off. Lying on my back, naked atop the sheets, my breath evened out and my thoughts began to fade into the star-speckled sky outside the castle windows.

I was just about to doze off when firm hands circled my ankles and pulled me to the edge of the bed. The round stud on Lyklor's tongue touched my clit—cool metal followed by his warm mouth. My moan woke me out of my light slumber. I sat up and took in the view of my mate on his knees between my legs. Digging my fingers into his thick, damp blond hair, I pulled his head in closer. Lyklor's tongue swirled and flicked, drawing more heat from my core. Gasping from the pleasure, I closed my eyes and threw my head back, squeezing Lyklor's head between my thighs.

"Um, that's not how babies are made." Ryo's voice came like a sudden wind gust beside us.

My eyes fluttered open. Lyklor cursed between my legs, drawing his head back.

Ryo stood in a black robe at the edge of the bed on Lyklor's left. I'd never heard him enter, which meant he must have dreamscaped.

"Why in the seven hells have you projected here? Now?" Lyklor demanded, getting to his feet.

Ah, so I had been correct.

"Checking in," Ryo said with casual nonchalance. "I miss you guys. Well, I mostly miss Mel." His projection smirked.

"Aw," I said, placing a hand to my heart. "We miss you too."

Lyklor grunted as he grabbed his pink robe and stuffed his arms into each sleeve. "Speak for yourself. I, for one, would like a little privacy. Is that not possible for one full day and night?"

Rather than answer, Ryo looked him up and down, smirked, and said, "Nice robe."

"Go away," Lyklor returned.

"I don't know." Ryo rubbed his jaw. "Maybe I should stay and supervise." He glanced down. "Looks like your cock could use some encouragement."

Pink robe open, Lyklor stood with his legs spread apart and semi-hard. He narrowed his eyes at Ryo. "What my cock needs is uninterrupted time with our mate. Your presence doesn't exactly inspire a hard-on, though I'm sure you're at full size beneath your robe."

"Let's see, shall we?" Grinning mischievously, Ryo undid the belt around his robe, allowing it to hang open.

So, yeah, I watched with eager eyes. My mates were gorgeous and well endowed. Fae males were more magical than unicorns (but don't tell Aerith I said so). I never tired of looking at either of them, and no, I didn't need anyone to draw me a picture. I got to enjoy the real deal up close and personal. I'd managed to snag a pair of gorgeous Fae kings.

Ryo was, as Lyklor had suggested, rock solid beneath his black robe. My lips parted as I drank him in with my eyes. Before I had a chance to bring the Russian roulette idea back to the table, Lyklor planted himself in front of me, blocking my view of Ryo.

"We made an agreement." Lyklor placed his hands on his hips. "If you continue to interrupt, then I'll call dibs for the rest of the year."

Ugh, not this dibs business again.

"Very well, no more interferences," Ryo said.

"And that goes for Reed and Ronin too."

"What about Lark?"

HOLIDAY CROWN

"He wouldn't dare."

It was the truth. Now in his fifteenth year, our golden prince had mellowed out. He was the most cultured of our family, with his music and dance lessons. More than his brothers, he tried to fit into Faerie.

"Fine," Ryo said. "But just so you know, I'll be in my room jacking off thinking about the two of you."

When Ryo disappeared, Lyklor groaned and covered his ears as though that would block out the images flooding in. Well, I don't know whether he was thinking about Ryo getting himself off, but I certainly was. My fingers slid up my thigh and stroked the wet heat between my legs.

With an animalistic growl, Lyklor captured my wrist and pinned it over my head. He thrust into me, clearly not that bothered by Ryo's spectral visit.

I wrapped my legs around Lyklor's muscled thighs and hooked my ankles above his hips. Eyes closed, I imagined Ryo jerking himself off and taking his release at the same time as Lyklor. I thought of my belly swollen, breasts heavy, and all the joy a baby girl would add to our family.

For some inexplicable reason, my mind told me to "think pink." Lyklor was really starting to rub off on me.

Faint sunlight filtered through my eyelids the next morning. I blinked several times, finding all the candles extinguished and Lyklor absent from our bed. I listened intently for sounds from the adjoining bathing chamber but heard nothing. As I swung one leg over the bed, a knock came at the door. I paused.

"Who is it?"

Rather than answer or give me time to fully cover myself with the blanket, Aerith burst into the room with a big, bright smile, looking way too cheerful for such an early hour. "Good morning, Mel!" she called out as she swept over to my bedside in a sky-blue cotton gown. Her hair was brushed out into a blonde shine loose over each shoulder.

"Morning? I think this still counts as night," I grumbled. Aerith just chuckled like I'd made a joke. "What are you doing here?" I asked. "Christmas isn't for another five weeks."

Taking a seat on the edge of my bed, Aerith's grin turned conspiratorial. "Lyklor visited me in a dreamscape and explained the situation."

"He what?" I clutched the blanket to my chest, eyebrows shooting to my hairline. So much for a Christmas surprise. My silver-tongued mate and I were going to have words. He had the ability to lie, yet he'd whisked himself away to Pinemist for a tell-all with my sister.

"Eeeeee! A baby girl. I'm so excited for you, Mel." Aerith pressed her hands together.

"Let's not get ahead of ourselves. We keep getting interrupted." I gave Aerith a pointed look. My sister stood and smoothed out her skirts, suddenly all business.

"That's why I'm here. Jhaeros, Fraya, and I are going to keep Ryo and the boys company while you and Lyklor go have some private time away from the castle." She leaned forward and winked.

Swell, now Jhaeros knew my business too. Then again, taking off on an adventure did sound appealing. I pursed my lips in thought.

"Where would Lyklor and I go?"

"That, Sister, is entirely up to you."

CHAPTER THREE

Aerith

The parlor was a flurry of activity as Reed and Ronin told me about their favorite rides at a place called Universal Studios in the mortal realm.

"Transformers was the best," Reed announced.

"No. Spider-Man was better," Ronin countered.

"Everyone knows Transformers beats Spider-Man."

I glanced at Jhaeros, who shrugged and said, "I have no idea what they're talking about," before returning to his adult conversation with Ryo and Folas. My raven-haired brother-in-law wore a gold crown encrusted with gems and was dressed in a black tailored tunic and breeches. Eight-year-old Gayla sat in an armchair near her father, head bent, doodling in a notebook.

After enjoying a delicious family breakfast, we were waiting for Mel and Lyklor to pack their bags and say goodbye before portaling somewhere a little more private and less chaotic.

"Auntie Aerith, Spider-Man landed on our vehicle and we dropped off a skyscraper." Ronin tugged at my skirt.

"That sounds exciting," I said.

Joining his brother's side, Reed made sure I understood that a skyscraper was way taller than the castle.

"Taller than anything you've ever seen in Pinemist," Ronin added. Reed nodded.

Now that the twins were back in agreement, they slunk away like a pair of jackals toward Fraya and Lark, who sat on a rug playing a board game called Ticket To Ride with little train car pieces they purchased with color-coded cards to complete routes across an area of the human world known as Europe.

Fraya and Lark were too busy studying the game board to notice the twins creeping up. Ronin snatched a green game piece from Fraya, and Reed took one of Lark's red train cars.

"Hey!" Lark yelled, his head snapping up.

"Choo-choo. All aboard the Hogwarts Express!" Reed announced before running across the room with Ronin.

Leaping to his feet, Lark took off after the pair. Fraya rolled her eyes, replaced the stolen piece with a new green train, then returned to studying the board and her cards. Yep, that was my daughter—no doubt about it. We'd played this game as a family back home. Thanks to Mel and her family's routine visits to the mortal realm, we'd been introduced to many new board games. Campaigne was still my favorite, but I didn't mind mixing it up, especially with games that allowed for more than two players. Earth definitely had some good things going for it, including Christmas . . . in particular, the cookies and treats. Puddings, fudge, and buttercream cupcakes. Gingerbread houses and candy canes—oh, sweet molasses and mint! My mouth watered just thinking about it.

"Boys, let Fraya and Lark play their game," Ryo said.

Ronin screeched when Lark caught hold of him and gave him a shake.

"Give it back now."

"Reed has it."

Reed stuck out his tongue at Lark. My nephew's eyes narrowed.

Fraya tossed her blonde hair back, turning her head to aim stern looks at Reed and Ronin. "You two do know what happens to naughty little boys at Christmas, don't you?" The twins exchanged a blank glance before turning their attention back to Fraya. She sighed dramatically. "Santa brings them coal rather than presents."

A smirk appeared over Lark's lips. He let go of Ronin. "No gifts for bad little boys," he taunted.

"That's not true," Reed said. "There is no Santa in Faerie."

"Santa can travel across realms," Fraya said with conviction. She set her cards facedown on the rug in front of the game board and tilted her head back.

Sixteen years old. She was growing up so fast—and taking after Keerla in fashion. Fraya wore a snug forest green bodysuit with long sleeves and a tight brown leather tunic with long loose flaps hanging around her slender legs. Fitted brown leather boots with cream branch embroidery hugged her calves up to her knees. They matched the arm cuffs from her wrists to her elbows.

My daughter had won countless archery tournaments in Pinemist—all with a seamless grace. She was never one to boast or show off. Jhaeros and I considered ourselves pretty dang lucky. Unfortunately, the young males of Pinemist had taken notice of Fraya, and that was something Jhaeros and I weren't ready for.

Ronin's lower lip quivered, on the verge of tears. The twins could go from hyper to sensitive within seconds. I offered Ronin a smile and softened my voice.

"Don't worry. I'll still give you presents," I told my raven-haired nephew.

His chin still trembled. Apparently, Santa's gifts held more appeal than Auntie Aerith's. I held back a chuckle.

"If you give the game pieces back now, I'm sure Santa will overlook your childish conduct," Fraya said.

"Santa might, but don't be so sure about Dad," Ryo said in a warning voice.

When Lark held out his open palm to Ronin, the younger boy pushed past him announcing, "I have cousin Fraya's train."

"You have to catch me if you want yours back," Reed informed his big brother.

Lark sprinted for his brother. Reed flashed past Ryo who tried, unsuccessfully, to grab him. Lark thundered after him in hot pursuit.

Not taking her eyes off her doodling, Gayla said, "I'm glad Fraya is here. Boys are so immature."

Folas met my eyes and sent me a look that seemed to say, "We have the only sensible children in the entire castle."

Lark caught up to Reed and wrenched his game piece from the young male's fingers.

"You nearly pulled off one of my fingers, you pit head," Reed sniped.

"Serves you right, infant." Lark returned to the rug, where he and Fraya bent their heads over the game board as though they'd never been interrupted.

Ryo rubbed the back of his neck and released a deep sigh.

Mel and Lyklor walked in hand in hand with glowing cheeks. I felt a tiny tug on my heart, wishing for a moment that we could all go on a couple's vacation. But this wasn't the time. Besides, Ryo clearly needed reinforcements. I understood Lyklor's request for time alone with my sister. I had no doubt they'd have success. As to whether they got the girl they wanted, that was up to Sky Mother, no matter what methods the blond Fae king attempted.

My bet was on a boy, mostly because Jhaeros was betting on a girl, and it wasn't fun if we bet on the same gender. Fraya was going with girl too. We hadn't had a chance to ask Folas if he wanted in on the bet. It was probably better to do it out of earshot of Ryo since he was as gung-ho as Lyklor to bring a daughter into the family. I hoped they got what they wanted, despite my bet.

HOLIDAY CROWN

"Well, kiddos, Mom and Dad are going away for a little while," Lyklor said.

"No!" Ronin yelled. He ran to Mel and wrapped his arms around her leg. She laughed and patted his head.

"We'll be back soon, and maybe we'll even find you some more presents."

Lyklor groaned in exasperation. "Don't you think we got them enough already?"

"There's always room for more," Reed said from his spot behind Gayla's chair. "What is that supposed to be?" he asked, peering over her shoulder.

Ronin let go of Mel's leg to hug her middle. She bent down and hugged him back. Ryo walked over and placed a reassuring hand on Ronin's shoulder.

"Behave yourselves while your father and I are away. See that crown on Dad's head? It means he's in charge and you must do as he says."

Ronin and Reed nodded simultaneously as though their heads were connected.

Jhaeros sidled up beside me and whispered, "Shouldn't they obey him even when he's not wearing a crown?"

"Maybe he lacks your natural authority," I whispered back.

Jhaeros's gaze dipped from my eyes to my lips, remaining on my mouth long enough for my thoughts to turn to passionate kisses. Maybe Dahlquist was all the vacation we needed.

33

"Reed, come give your mother a hug," Mel said. He went right over. The boys were good at listening when it came to Mel. Elf mamas weren't to be messed with. Squeezing a twin in each arm, Mel pulled them closer and blinked several times. "You too, Lark. I want a hug from all my boys before I go."

Lark smacked his palm to his forehead and groaned. "Mom, we're in the middle of a game. I'll see you again soon."

"Lark," Lyklor said in a warning tone.

Releasing the twins, Mel sauntered over to her firstborn, squinting down at the game. "Lately the two of you do nothing but play these games for hours. You know we have a whole armory filled with sharp pointy objects, right?"

Fraya looked up and smiled sweetly. "No, thanks, Aunt Mel."

"We're good," Lark added.

"Ugh." Mel turned to me. "Please don't turn my son into a gaming nerd."

"Too late," I replied with a smirk.

She huffed at me before returning her attention to Lark.

"Up. Up. Up. I'm not leaving until I get my hug."

Lark got up and gave her a quick hug. Mel pulled him back and squeezed him extra long and tight.

"Mom, you're crushing me."

Reed snickered.

"Where's my hug?" Ryo asked.

Mel threw her arms around her raven-haired mate. Their hug stretched on before ending with a passionate kiss.

Once Mel released Ryo, I stepped in to hug her, whispering, "Good luck, Little Sis."

"Where are you headed?" Jhaeros asked.

"Secret location." Lyklor's voice rose across the room.

Smiling, Mel leaned in closer, lowering her voice. "Dubai. We're going skydiving over the Palm Islands." She bounced on the balls of her toes. Seeing our blank expressions, Mel stopped bouncing and groaned. "I'll just have to send postcards so you can see for yourself."

Turning to Jhaeros, I tapped my lower lip. "Or maybe we should pop in for a visit." My mate snorted. Before Mel could protest, I gave her a loving pat on the shoulder. "Just remember to spend time in the hotel too. You've got business to take care of, after all."

Jhaeros took that as his cue to drift away and rejoin the males. Like Mel, he wasn't much for the public sex talks.

Trunks were carried down by servants after Mel and Lyklor took their leave. The rest of us got to work digging out garlands and faerie twinkle lights. We started with the family parlor then moved on to the halls of Dahlquist, concentrating on the most traversed passageways between the dining room, parlor, ballroom, and family suites.

Folas carried the ladder around, propping it against walls for Jhaeros to climb as I held garland to his awaiting hands.

Might as well get into the spirit. According to Hensley, the holidays went into high gear beginning the week of an American holiday called Thanksgiving, which was fast approaching. I hadn't seen much of my human sister-in-law over the years, but that was okay. Liri was far from my favorite in-law, and I imagined that wouldn't change. At least I was able to tolerate him, especially barely seeing him. It turned out Hensley was barren, but she said she didn't mind, especially with her passion for theater to keep her occupied. Liri didn't care either. Given he'd killed his own father to obtain the crown, it was little wonder. Liri had never struck me as father material. Luckily, Lyklor and Ryo didn't take after him that way. Nope, Liri was his own special breed of creature.

"That's the last of it," I said as Jhaeros hooked the remaining bit of garland along the wall leading to the dining room.

He climbed down the ladder. Folas left it propped against the wall, and we returned to the parlor, where we found ornaments covering all the available chairs, sofa, and countertops.

The servants were still carrying down trunks. Lulu and her adopted son, Alok, carried the next one in together and looked around for an empty spot.

"I think I saw space in the corner," Jhaeros said, taking the handle from Lulu.

"Thank you," she chirped.

With Jhaeros's height, the side Alok carried dipped down. The young male was Lark's age. He had black hair with blue highlights. Lulu had once made them purple, which Lark had teased him relentlessly over. Lark had mellowed out over the years, but he wasn't great at making friends besides Fraya and Devdan's daughter, Zelie, back in Pinemist. I was happy to see Fraya get along so well with her cousins.

The trunk bumped against the floor when Jhaeros and Alok released it. Lifting the lid, Jhaeros looked inside and said, "Well, we found Mel's collection of holiday picture books."

"What are we supposed to do with all these ornaments?" Gayla asked. She'd abandoned her doodling to help pull decorations from the trunks.

"We need a tree," Reed said.

"There are some fake ones in the attic," Lulu said.

"We should go out and cut down a real tree," I said.

"A real tree!" Reed and Ronin said in unison, jumping up and down.

Ryo rubbed his jaw. "Sounds like fun, but I can't leave the castle. We could send Folas to bring back a tree." Ryo lowered his hand and looked at the blond guard. Folas nodded his consent.

"No! We want to pick out the tree," Ronin said. "Uncle Jhaeros will take us, won't you?"

Jhaeros shrugged. "I don't see why not."

"I'll go too," I said. "Fraya?" I asked my daughter, who stood near a trunk untangling faerie lights.

"I'll stay at the castle," she said, continuing to unwind copper wiring.

"I'll stay as well," Lark announced.

"Shouldn't you go along and look after your brothers?" Fraya suggested.

Lark's face fell. He sighed and gave the twins a cursory glance. "I suppose."

"Or maybe you need me to come along, being the oldest and all," she teased.

"Only by six months." Lark put his hands on his hips.

"It's settled then. Jhaeros and I will take the boys out to find the perfect Christmas tree."

"I'll accompany you, along with half-a-dozen royal guards," Folas said. "Gayla, you stay here with Fraya." His daughter looked at Fraya and smiled widely.

"Want to hang out in my room and color?"

"Maybe later. I want to untangle these lights," Fraya said.

Gayla's face fell, similar to Lark's. My daughter was Miss Popular whenever our families got together. Her friends back home were always coming by seeking her company. She had a natural magnetic pull that made others want to be around her. The boy thing was the problem. At least Fraya wasn't a flirt. Then again, that only seemed to make the males scramble to win her affections all the more. As with everything, I trusted my daughter to behave herself.

I should have known it wouldn't last.

CHAPTER FOUR

Fraya

I kept my attention on the task of untangling faerie lights as my parents left the parlor with Folas and my cousins.

The sound of breaking glass sent all eyes to Gayla, who cringed as she stood over a shattered reindeer ornament.

"I'm sorry!" she cried. "It fell out of my hand."

"There, there. We have plenty more," Uncle Ryo said, going straight to Gayla and bending on one knee to give her a gentle pat. I swear he doted on her more than her own father did. Folas was the stoic sort. A loyal guard and reliable parent where his mate had failed.

Gayla stared at my uncle's head. "We should decorate your crown for Christmas," she said.

Uncle Ryo chuckled and touched the golden circlet. "Do you think a bit of garland would make it more festive?"

Gayla nodded eagerly. She always brought out my smile. She was such a cute, sweet little Fae girl.

Getting up and taking her hand, my uncle led her toward the open doors. "Let's see if we can find some in the hallway."

My heart rate kicked up as they left. I hurried with the lights, which weren't that bad to begin with, and rewound them into tidy loops.

"These are ready," I announced, avoiding eye contact with Alok as I set the lights on the armrest of a chair filled with ornaments. "I'll see if there are any more decorations in the attic."

"We got them all, Miss Fraya," Lulu said.

"Wonderful. Thank you, Lulu. I suppose there's not much else to be done until they return with the tree." I swept out of the room.

Reaching the corridor, I took off in the opposite direction of my uncle and Gayla. Luckily, they were preoccupied as Uncle Ryo lifted Gayla up, and she yanked pieces of greenery from a wreath. They looked so cute. I hoped he and Uncle Lyklor got the daughter they were hoping for. Whatever the gender, I was excited to cuddle my new baby cousin in my arms. I loved all my cousins, and since my aunt Shalendra didn't want kids, I was happy Aunt Mel had grown her family.

I wanted kids one day. Two seemed like a good number—a girl and a boy a few years apart. But that was years away, of course, after I was an adult and had become archery champion of the elven realm. If I lived on Earth, I'd have shelves lined with trophies and ribbons. Elves had no need for awards. Reputation was enough. But that hadn't stopped Aunt Mel from having one made up for me during one of her routine trips to the mortal realm. She'd had my name engraved on a gold-toned plate attached to the base of a metal shield with a target and arrows jutting out of the bull's-eye in the middle. It was one of my favorite gifts and sat on the middle of my shelf in my room back in Pinemist. Aunt Mel was the best! It was no wonder she'd snagged the hearts of two Fae males.

I'd recently discovered the appeal of the Fae. I'd kissed a couple of elves back home. They were nice males, though hesitant and awkward, looking to me for direction. I liked a male to take charge. The Fae took charge. One in particular.

My heart rate quickened.

Alok was waiting for me in the attic when I walked into the narrow space located above the castle's ballroom. Light filtered in through a single window, catching the brilliant blue highlights in his midnight hair. He was more gorgeous than any male I'd ever seen in the elven realms or Faerie.

I put my hands on my hips. "Did you portal here?" I'd meant to beat him to our meeting spot.

With his back to the small square window, Alok's face was shadowed, making his smile appear dangerous. There had always been a dark energy surrounding him like a black hole. Looking at him, heat radiated from my neck to my core all the way down to each toe bound by my leather boots.

"Maybe, or maybe I'm just faster." He smiled deviously.

I scowled. The rogue knew how competitive I was. I thought only Fae royals and their chosen guards were capable of portaling, but there was still so much I didn't know about Faerie. Alok must have raced here the moment I headed out.

Sadly, Fae trumped elves in speed. At least he was as eager as I.

"I've missed you, Fraya." The longing in Alok's voice pulled me toward him.

We met in the middle of the attic, grabbing one another roughly. I fisted Alok's black tunic near his neck as he gripped me around my waist. Midnight black hair spilled over his forehead as though to eclipse the preternatural glow in his penetrating brown eyes.

I breathed in bergamot along with faint hints of lemon, ginger, sage, fir, and cedar musk. The smell of him drew out a wildness deep within me.

I'd missed Alok too—more than I was willing to admit out loud. I missed him every time one of the males back home tried to flirt or show off. They were like dull smudges compared to Alok's dark pulsating energy. I longed for him to appear inside my bed chamber at night, even in a dreamscape if only to see and speak to him in the stolen hours before sleep. Father's entire estate was heavily warded against dreamscaping. Mom had a special room only Uncle Ryo, Uncle Lyklor, or Folas could access if they needed to contact her.

We were worlds apart, and my need for him only grew more desperate after each absence.

Digging my fingers into his back, my hungry lips covered his. With a flick of his tongue, Alok drew out a strangled moan from low in my throat. Our kiss deepened, tongues pushing past teeth to plunder with savage demand.

HOLIDAY CROWN

Alok's deft fingers slipped up my sides to my shoulders. His lips moved from my mouth to my neck. I tilted my head back, eyes fluttering closed as I exposed my throat to him. I wanted to both surrender to him and conquer him in one breath. Never one to shy away, Alok's teeth scraped along my neck, his tongue tracing my collarbone, feeding the furnace inside my belly. Flames descended and pulsed between my thighs.

My body responded in kind. Heady arousal turned to sleek heat that bloomed inside my sex. There was nowhere to breathe inside the tight bodysuit. The attic felt like it was tightening us in together, cocooning me and Alok in a lovers' embrace.

I only wanted more. More kisses. More friction. More of him.

We might as well have portaled into the middle of the galaxy. There was only Alok, a dark, carnal mass of swirling desire. My body trembled against him. The castle and the attic faded. There was nothing beyond the dampness soaking through my snug body suit and the empty ache high above my thighs.

I pressed my body into his lean fame, wanting to hear him groan with need. At fifteen, Alok was tall, trim, and already toned with muscles from endless activity at the castle. My first memory of him was as a sulky child after he was first adopted, but Lulu's love and his life at Dahlquist had shaped him into the robust and mature young male he'd become.

The first time we kissed, he said he was going to marry me one day. I'd found his declaration both amusing and naively romantic. But the more time I spend with Alok, the more I feel like a starfish caught in a whirlpool.

His arm circled my waist. Bold fingers from his second hand stroked my thigh then cupped me between the legs. The warmth of his fingers spread through the tight material of my bodysuit. I rubbed shamelessly against his hand until he worked his thumb over my aching, tender folds. The steady friction generated bolts of pleasure rippling along my thighs. My desire seeped through the fabric pants, permeating the dank attic air and dampening Alok's finger where he stroked.

We stumbled over to a pile of blankets I suspected Alok had arranged before my arrival.

I climbed on top of Alok and rubbed against the hard length straining beneath his tunic and trousers. Our kisses grew sloppy as we gyrated over the attic floor. With a gasp and a pant, I broke off the kiss and sat upright over the beautiful Fae male.

"I want you to be my first," I told him. I'd given it a lot of consideration. Like my mom, I was a planner. I wasn't sure she ever planned this sort of thing, though. According to my parents, they hadn't even liked each other when they first met.

Alok and I didn't have a lot of opportunities together. My family only ever came to Dahlquist when Aunt Mel was in residence, and even then, our visits were rare. Mom preferred to spend time with her sister when she was in Pinemist.

I'd been craving this for months. Living a realm away, unable to talk or touch, was torture.

Alok gazed at me with eyes that shimmered in the dark. "Are you sure?" he asked. "You know I'll wait for you, Fraya."

I dipped down and gave him a quick, hard kiss.

"I don't want to wait." I smiled. "Do you know someone who can procure a tincture after and be discreet?"

Unlike Aunt Mel, I didn't want a swollen belly stretching my leathers in the new year.

"Lulu. She's a romantic. She would never say a word."

I twisted my lips to the side, not sure how eager I was for Lulu to know our business. She was a sweet, if simple, female, not the sort to flash me knowing smiles. I certainly preferred this option a thousand times over to asking Mrs. Calarel, our cook back in Pinemist. She'd run straight to my parents and find a way to tell them, despite being deaf.

"Okay," I said.

Alok's intense stare made me ache with anticipation. I'd spent the past year wondering what it would feel like to have sex. It was like an unfinished puzzle driving me crazy with the urge to complete. The big question would soon be answered.

"I'll sneak into your room tonight," Alok whispered as though he was already tiptoeing his way to my guest chamber.

"Let's do it now," I said.

"Now?" His eyes widened. "Here? In the attic?"

A taunting smile lifted my lips. "Unless you really want to wait," I said sweetly before rocking my hips over his.

Alok's eyes squeezed shut, and I was pleased to get a moan out of him. He pulled me down and rolled us over, reversing our positions so he was on top.

"I want you to be my first too," he rasped, grinding against me. "You're the only female I've ever wanted to mate with."

"Flatterer." I chuckled.

"You know I can't lie." Alok growled.

That was something I did know, and it sent surges of electric bliss straight to my ego.

"I want you and no other," Alok continued. "I wanted you from the moment I saw you, Fraya Keasandoral. One day, I want to claim you as my life mate."

"Let's not get ahead of ourselves," I scolded, even as my belly did flips. I was nowhere near ready to settle down. Alok's fervor still surprised me. I would have thought a fifteen-year-old Fae male would want to keep his options open. Maybe there was a bit of a romantic in me because his proclamations were making my heart go gooey. But I was still practical. And curious. And ready to have sex for the first time.

I'd chosen a difficult outfit for getting undressed. We were still dry humping one another through our clothing, kissing, panting, and gasping so loud that we never heard the intruder until he roared in outrage and yanked Alok off.

Alok fell over a wood chair and hit the ground several feet away. Lark stood over him, fingers curled into fists, and murder glittering in his blue eyes.

"Get up, you piece of filth!" Lark bellowed.

Alok lifted himself off the ground and held his head high as though he was the prince and Lark the underling. Both males glared at one another with a deep hatred that chilled my heart.

I got to my feet and hugged my arms around my middle, feeling sick to my stomach at being discovered and witnessing my cousin's violent reaction.

"You think a lowly servant such as yourself has the right to touch my cousin?" Lark sneered.

"I'm not a servant," Alok said through clenched jaw.

"Son of a servant. Not even her son. An orphan." Lark's upper lip curled.

"I. Am. Not. The. Son. Of. A. Servant." Conviction and pride stamped each word Alok enunciated.

"I will have you and your servant mother out of the castle before nightfall," Lark said with a cruel smile.

"Lark!" I snapped.

Ignoring me, my cousin folded his arms and lifted his nose, looking down at Alok.

The dark-haired Fae returned his cold grin. "You are not king of the castle. And you're just jealous that Fraya wants me, not you. It's pathetic."

Lark's face contorted in rage. "Fraya's my cousin, you sick piece of shit."

"*I'm* the one who's sick?" Alok taunted.

"I don't think of Fraya that way. She's family."

This confrontation was getting way out of hand. I didn't appreciate Alok trying to sully my close friendship with Lark by making lewd suggestions.

"I wonder, does your elf blood make it possible for you to lie, halfling, or is your tongue pierced like your father's?" Alok raised his dark brows.

With a roar, Lark launched himself at Alok, getting in the first hit. They grabbed one another between punches, ending up on the ground, rolling around trading blows. My heart lurched up like the model rocket Aunt Mel had brought back to Pinemist on her last visit.

"Lark, stop!"

Lark grabbed Alok by his head and slammed it against the floor.

Normally my cousin listened to me. Being so blatantly ignored had me blinking several times.

"Stop!" I said louder.

Alok pushed Lark aside and kicked him.

Footsteps pounded up the stairs.

"What's going on up here?"

My racing heart slowed and stuttered to a stop as my father entered the attic.

Oh, pitberries.

His voice inspired the males to separate and pick themselves up off the floor. My father glowered, looking

HOLIDAY CROWN

between them. The hard lines of his jaw tightened. "Why were you two fighting?" he demanded.

My stomach bottomed out, sure that Lark would sing like a canary. But my cousin pressed his lips together in defiance. We weren't just family; we were best friends. His steadfast loyalty touched my heart despite his cruel treatment toward Alok. Lark was only trying to look out for me. I didn't have a brother. He was the closest thing to one.

"Lark?" My father's deep voice filled me with dread.

Lark said nothing.

"Alok, do you want to tell me what happened?" Dad asked, casting the dark-haired Fae a look of contention.

Taking his cue from Lark, Alok admitted to nothing. Instead, he narrowed his eyes at Lark and said, "You have no idea who I am," before storming out.

"A low-class pit head, that's who," Lark called after him.

My father crossed his arms over his chest and narrowed his eyes on Lark. "Very well, nephew. You refuse to speak. At least I can count on Fraya to tell me the truth. You can go now."

I grimaced. Face mottled red, Lark still managed to shoot me an apologetic look before slinking out of the room.

My father's eyes locked on mine.

"Aren't you supposed to be out finding a tree?" I asked.

"Don't change the subject."

Yikes, my dad could be really intimidating when he wanted. My forehead wrinkled. Taking a deliberate look around the attic, my father's focus zeroed in on the pile of rumpled blankets on the floor. My next breath caught in my chest. A tight frown appeared over my father's face.

"I'm not blind, Fraya."

Yeah, too bad our butler, Fhaornik, hadn't walked in. Then there would have been nothing to see or report back on.

"Did you and Alok have sex?"

Gah! Straight to the point. I wished my mom was the one who had found us. My cheeks were flaming redder than Rudolph's nose.

"No." I should have left it at that, but teenage rebellion rose up in me when I added, "We were interrupted before we had a chance to get that far."

Oh, Sweet Sky. Way to go, Fraya.

My father's nostrils flared, and his head jerked.

"And what of the consequences?" he demanded. "Are you ready to have a child? How would you feel stuck at home nursing a baby while your friends were out touring the realm, competing in tournaments?"

"I was going to drink a tincture afterward. I'm not stupid."

"That is debatable," he said without missing a beat.

Had my father just insulted me? My mouth gaped open. Tears stung my eyes. I was mortified when I felt the first wet tear track down my cheek. More leaked out. I tried to hide my face. Unlike some of my female friends back home, I never wanted my parents to see me cry—not even to get out of trouble.

My father's face fell, his shoulders dropping. "Fraya." He whispered my name with love and anguish.

"I don't want to talk to you," I said, storming past him. I flew down the narrow stairwell to the corridor below, tears blurring my vision as I ran to my room where I flung myself onto the bed, burying my tear-soaked face into the covers.

Sometime later, a light tapping came at the door.

"Go away," I called.

"Fraya, it's your mother."

Ugh, this day was getting suckier by the minute. I remained facedown on the bed as my mom entered my chamber, shutting the door behind her. Soft footsteps approached the bed. I waited impatiently for her to expand on my father's disappointment, but my mom said nothing.

Unable to take the silence for long, I turned around and gaped when I saw my mom's face splotchy from crying.

"Mom! Nothing happened."

"I know," she said softly, bowing her head. "I'm just not ready for you to grow up. I know I cannot slow the hands of time, but it feels like just yesterday you were my baby girl and we had all the time in the world together." Mom's voice cracked, and tears spilled down her cheeks. Her tears made me start crying again.

I scrambled out of bed and wrapped my arms around my mother. "I'm still your baby girl," I said through tears.

"I know," Mom said, hugging me, but her tone was one of resignation and heartache.

"Mom!" I said again. Oh my Sky, she was making me feel worse than Father.

She sniffled and pulled my head against her shoulder.

"Look, maybe I was rushing things. I was just curious, but I can probably wait a few more years."

"That long?" Mom pulled back and looked at me. A second later, we erupted into a fit of laughter. It made me want to cry all over again because I had the best mother in all the realms, and the best father—even if he thought I was an idiot.

"Why didn't you go get a tree?" I asked, ready to change the subject. I stepped away from my mom and wrapped my fingers around my leather wrist cuff.

"Oh," Mom said as though she'd forgotten all about the abandoned trek. "After your father grabbed an ax from the armory, Lark insisted you would want to help chop down the tree. He was convinced you'd come along if he asked you one more time."

Pitberries. I felt so bad. Stupid hormones making things awkward for everyone. From here on out, I'd get a handle over myself—keep it to kissing. I could wait. I just wished Lark hadn't called Alok a servant. I think deep down my cousin struggled with his sense of self-confidence. His fathers shared the throne with his uncle Liri. He wasn't full-Fae, nor was he a full-time resident of Dahlquist. But he was the kingdom's firstborn prince. The situation wasn't typical, even in a place like Faerie, so I imagined it could be confusing.

HOLIDAY CROWN

"How am I going to face everyone at dinner?" I groaned into my hands.

"Your father and I are the only ones who know . . . well, us and Lulu and, of course, Lark and Alok."

"Dad thinks I'm a dummy," I said with a pout.

"No, he doesn't. He's just having a hard time accepting that you're growing up. Harder than I am," Mom added with a sad smile.

"What will happen to Alok?" My heart twisted thinking of the gorgeous Fae. I already imagined my parents would keep us apart, but I didn't want him or Lulu to be tossed out as Lark had threatened.

Mom cleared her throat. "Lulu arranged for him to work in the stable. We agreed it was best if he wasn't around the family."

My heart sank. The position was much lower than aiding his mother in the castle. Alok would hate mucking out stalls and feeding animals.

"It's for the best," Mom repeated, seeing the look on my face.

Not for Alok, I wanted to say. It was my fault he'd been banished to the stables. I had to find a way to sneak out and apologize. I should be the one sleeping in the hay. I'd been the one to proposition him. Ugh. It was so unfair. Total class bias. I couldn't care less whether Alok was a servant or a secret Fae prince. To me, he was marvelous—a male who could make me laugh, yearn, and glow from within. I still wanted him to be my first. We'd just have to wait. Well, *I* would have to wait. I didn't expect him to. I wasn't naïve. I understood males had biological needs. Perhaps he would forget all about Fraya the elf once he bedded a few of the castle's pretty faeries. My heart sank. I hoped that wouldn't be the case, even though it would be better for everyone.

CHAPTER FIVE

Aerith

Back and forth, Jhaeros paced our guest chamber, wearing a path into the rug. "I should take her home at once," he said.

"The situation is dealt with," I countered from the plush armchair where I sat with a decorative pillow in my lap. I couldn't stop tugging at the beaded tassels.

Coming to an abrupt halt, Jhaeros turned to me with an incredulous look. "They were about to have sex on the attic floor. What's to stop them from a romp in the hay?"

I lifted my chest. "Fraya assured me she intends to wait at least several years."

"And you believe her?"

I narrowed my eyes. "Yes, Jhaeros, I do. I trust our daughter."

"I used to," he said with a huff.

I stopped fiddling with the tassels and folded my hands on top of the pillow. "Even if they had gone all the way, it wouldn't have been the end of the world. It's going to happen one day."

"One day doesn't have to be today!" Jhaeros snapped. "I'm taking her home after dinner, and that's final."

Ohhh. I don't think so.

I stood up and threw the pillow at my bullheaded mate. His eyes rounded in surprise. I closed in on him, getting directly in front of his face so he could feel my hot breath. "Remember who you are speaking to. I'm not your daughter. I'm your mate. We make decisions together."

Jhaeros's lips lifted over his teeth. He looked ready to bite. Dark brown eyes traveled down my neck to my chest before snapping back up. I recognized the hungry look in his eyes. He couldn't decide whether he wanted to fight with me or fuck me.

Anticipation fluttered like snowflakes through my belly. If anyone was getting lucky tonight, it should be the adults. All those pent-up emotions had to go someplace.

I was pretty sure my mate would relent to a quickie before supper, but Folas burst into our chamber. If it hadn't been for his harried, wild appearance, I would have yelled at his intrusion.

"What's happened?" Jhaeros asked.

"It's Malon," Folas said, pressing his fists to the sides of his head. "He's escaped from the dungeons."

"What?" I screeched.

I'd forgotten all about the evil cousin Liri kept imprisoned beneath the castle. We'd all advised him against such idiocy, which had only strengthened his resolve. The white-haired king said it pleased him to think of the black-haired miscreant rotting away in a dark cell.

"How did he get loose?" Jhaeros asked, sounding way too calm. I was sure his heart had to be racing inside that delectably chiseled chest of his.

"It looks like someone let him out," Folas replied. "The dungeon guards were all asleep. Someone must have used sleeping powder."

"We need to portal the children out immediately," Jhaeros said, heading for the door.

"We can't," Folas said miserably.

Jhaeros and I gaped at the blond guard.

"Liri took precautions. He had the castle spelled to shut down all portals in or out of Dahlquist should Malon ever escape his cell." Folas shook his head.

Fucking Liri. He'd endangered my family yet again while he was conveniently stuffing his face with mashed potatoes and gravy in the mortal realm. Hensley had told me all about the holiday feasting. I hoped he choked on a cranberry.

"I'm going to kill him," I seethed.

"First, we have to catch him," Folas said. "But when we do, we should dispose of him once and for all."

"Not Malon. Liri," I said.

Folas pursed his lips. "But yeah, Malon needs to go too."

After tossing ornaments out of the way, our family squeezed together on the sofas and chairs, sequestered inside the parlor. Reed and Ronin sat on either side of Ryo on one sofa. Across from them, Gayla pressed against Fraya. I sat on the edge of an armchair with Jhaeros standing at my side. Folas stood behind his daughter, and Lark leaned against the sofa near his brothers.

Folas had two dozen guards stationed outside the parlor and another ten inside with us. It was difficult to appreciate the security when I felt like a sitting duck.

"I'm going to hunt him down," I said, getting to my feet.

"You stay. I'll go," Jhaeros said.

"I know this castle as well as any Elmray," I countered.

"You don't really mean to go out there, do you?" Fraya asked, her face blanching.

Folas folded his arms across his chest. "We need to stay and protect the children."

"That's what you are for, Folas," I said. "Someone helped him. For all we know, it's a sorcerer. They could blow more of their sleeping dust over the guards outside. We have to find them and stop them before they get to us."

Folas shook his head. "The castle is warded against sorcerers. I would have known if one tried to cross through."

Well, that was one relief. Isadore had given me a lifelong fear of sorcery.

Ryo puffed out his chest. "I am acting king. I will go."

"That's exactly why you have to stay here," I said, whirling around to face him.

HOLIDAY CROWN

"Not this again." Ryo scoffed.

"If not for your kingdom, then for your boys." I lifted my brows.

Ryo didn't argue.

"We already have guards looking for him," Folas said, his arms still tightly wrapped around his broad chest.

"And if we're lucky, they'll find him first, but I'm not waiting around to find out." I turned to my daughter next. "Keep the children calm until we get back. I don't plan on allowing Malon anywhere near this parlor, but if any enemy should get through, don't hesitate to take him down."

A bow and quiver filled with arrows rested on the low table in front of Fraya. There wasn't an elf in all the realms who could outshoot my daughter. Right before gathering, Folas, Jhaeros, and I had grabbed as many weapons as our arms could carry from the armory before locking it up and stationing more guards at its doors.

My daughter said nothing, merely nodded, a tight frown on her face.

"Do not hesitate," I repeated. I looked at Jhaeros next. We started out of the parlor.

"Wait," Fraya called, running toward us. She hugged me tightly. I wrapped my beautiful girl in my arms and gave her a final squeeze. Once we let go, Fraya looked at her toes then gave Jhaeros an uncertain look.

"No hug for your dad?" he asked softly.

Like that, a smile spread over Fraya's lips, and she launched herself into her father's arms. "Be safe," Fraya commanded.

"You too," Jhaeros said.

I grabbed a bow and quiver filled with arrows near the door. Jhaeros picked up one of the swords. We gave our family one final look of farewell before entering the hall.

"Didn't even get to eat dinner first," I grumbled as we clipped along toward the royal wing. Malon was going to have one hangry elf on his hands. I loved this word "hangry" Mel had taught me from the mortal realm. It was fitting right now.

Given the sense of entitlement Albedo and Malon had expressed previously over the kingdoms of Dahlquist and Ravensburg, I reasoned that the best place to begin our search was the royal chambers. Perhaps we'd find him trying on Liri's crowns.

Torchlight flickered along the dark corridor, sending shadows skittering over the stone floor like spiders. Flame reflected off the blade Jhaeros carried at his side. Guards in green-and-gold tunics were stationed throughout. They watched as we passed. Once we located Malon, we'd have backup at the ready. I couldn't imagine how the miscreant would move about the castle when there were guards everywhere. After the initial shock of his escape, I'd calmed myself, knowing it was only a matter of rounding up the Fae bastard and locking him back in his cage to await a swift execution. Who would do it? Ryo? Could he kill his own blood brother? Lyklor? He'd grown up believing Malon was his brother, though. Would he hesitate to end him permanently? Liri, of course, had no qualms over killing family, which made it all the more infuriating that he'd allowed Malon to live.

My palms turned clammy as we approached the two guards standing at the double doors that led into the open corridor of the south wing. My grip on the bow I carried loosened then tightened as I adjusted my hold on my weapon of choice. I hadn't visited the royal wing in seventeen years. The last time I was there, I'd been pregnant with Fraya, ruling Dahlquist in Liri's absence. That was before my sister claimed Ryo and Lyklor as mates and agreed to share the throne with Liri.

"Has anyone come through here tonight?" Jhaeros asked one of the guards.

"Only a couple servants, but every one of them came back out," the guard to the left answered.

As the guards pulled the doors open, I stared into the moonlight passageway and hesitated. Did I really want to waste time looking around this part of the castle? Now that I thought about it, the stables made more sense. Malon would want to try to escape Dahlquist altogether. I wasn't worried about him lurking in the royal wing so much as facing the ghosts of years past.

Jhaeros inched in closer to me, the warmth of his body reaching for mine. "What are you thinking?" he asked gently.

"I'm thinking we should start with the stables."

He nodded. "Let's check it out."

The halls were eerily quiet. It reminded me of a holiday story Mel read to the boys every December about the night before Christmas and no creatures stirring in the house, not even a mouse. In our case, it was a castle, and we were after a rat.

After passing another set of guards, Jhaeros sighed and ran his free hand over his head. "I'm not ready for Fraya to be interested in males."

Back to that. Malon wasn't the only scary thing we were dealing with.

"I'm not either," I admitted.

My mate turned his head, studying my face. "But you sounded so accepting of it earlier."

"I had to force myself to sound calm and understanding. I don't want our daughter doing that stuff when she's still so young."

"I don't want her doing it ever," Jhaeros muttered.

Poor Jhaeros. The days of sweet innocence were over. I was resigned to it, but I had a feeling Jhaeros would struggle through the remainder of Fraya's teenage years . . . and beyond.

"I hoped if I was open, she would be more likely to hold off," I reasoned. "When I warned Mel away from Devdan, she ran straight for him. Maybe my acceptance will work as reverse psychology."

"Or maybe we should lock her in her room until she turns thirty."

I snorted. "Sure, that will—" My sentence was cut off by shouting that resounded along the stone corridors.

Jhaeros and I took one look at each other then launched forward, running toward the commotion. It was a way off, the eager voices mere echoes as we raced toward them.

We rounded a corner, guards joining us. Boots pounded over the hard ground. My shimmery blue slippers didn't make any noise—there was enough of that all around me. My heart raced right alongside the group, eager anticipation coursing through me.

Around the next corner, we glimpsed sight of guards circling something we couldn't see at the end of the hall.

They'd caught him! I was sure of it. I hopped up in excitement then rushed forward with the rest of our group. We slowed to a jog as we neared. Ryo and Folas had come out of the parlor and were standing inside the circle. Guards parted at our approach.

"Did we catch him?" I asked breathlessly.

My answer lay bleeding on the ground. Sixteen years in the dungeon hadn't done Malon any favors. His cheeks were sunken in, a yellowish tint to his pale skin, tattered dark tunic, and matted and grimy black hair. He didn't look like any sort of serious threat, especially dead of multiple stab wounds.

My elation drifted back down like a kite shot through with an arrow. "Why is he dead?" I demanded. There would be no learning the identity of his accomplice now. Pitberries!

The guards nearest Malon twisted in place, looking at one another for someone to speak. Several licked their lips but said nothing. Finally, one of the guards cleared his throat and spoke up. "He was going to use magic faerie dust on us. We stopped him before he could."

"You did well," Ryo said with approval. "All of you. It was the right move."

Folas nodded beside him, grim satisfaction pressing over his lips.

A slight quiver ran through my stomach. I jerked around, feeling as though I was being watched. There were no eyes on me that I could see, but that didn't stop the hairs from prickling along the back of my neck.

"Where are the children?" I asked.

"Safe in the parlor," Folas answered.

I took off at a swift clip, Jhaeros and Folas hurrying after me. My heart pounded up my throat as I rushed into the parlor. The kids were all there, huddled together, watching the door. Gayla clung to Fraya's side. My daughter's face lit up when she saw me.

"What's going on out there?"

"Malon is dead," Jhaeros said. He went to our daughter, crouched down, and hugged her along with Gayla.

Gayla squirmed away and ran to Folas. "Daddy," she yelped, launching herself into Folas's muscled arms. It was sweet to see the bulky guard with his little girl. I'd never heard him take a sharp tone with her—not once.

HOLIDAY CROWN

When Ryo entered, Reed and Ronin left Lark's side to jump up and down in front of their dad.

"I want to see the dead body," Reed announced.

"Me too," Ronin said.

Ryo winced.

"Is there a lot of blood?" Reed pressed.

I cleared my throat. "Ryo, can I talk to you?" I motioned for Jhaeros and Folas to join us in a corner of the parlor. "Fraya, Lark, watch after the kids a moment before I speak with the two of you."

The teenagers nodded. A second later, I heard Lark snap, "No, you're not going to see the body. You're staying right here."

In the corner of the parlor, I huddled close to the males I'd called over, lowering my voice to a whisper. "Did the guards catch a glimpse of his accomplice?"

Ryo shook his head, the gold crown with its festive embellishments moving with him. "Unfortunately, he was alone, raving like a lunatic from what I heard. Probably went mad from all those years in the dungeon. They found powder on him. The guards had no choice but to strike first before he had a chance to blow it over them."

I rubbed the bridge of my nose. Even with Malon dead, I couldn't relax or find relief. "What about the individual who freed him?" I wanted to know.

"Now that Malon's dead, he—or she—will probably try to flee the castle. Whoever it was clearly needed Malon, otherwise they wouldn't have bothered risking his release.

They no longer have their powder to help them either," Ryo added. "There wasn't much left on Malon. His accomplice probably used most of it on the guards. The dust isn't easy to come by."

I squeezed the bow in my fist. "We'll have to question everyone in the castle," I said.

Ryo nodded and glanced toward the kids.

"I don't want to worry them," I said. "We'll tell Fraya and Lark, but not the little ones. They should stay together in adjoining chambers. Jhaeros and Folas can supervise the kids with the help of Fraya and Lark while Ryo and I question everyone in the castle."

Oh joy. This was going to take all night.

We were all quiet as we looked at the kids. Lark stared back with furrowed brows until his attention was pulled away by Reed pretending to stab Ronin with an invisible dagger. When his fist bumped into Ronin's chest, the twin gave a bellow of outrage and the two started shoving one another. Lark jumped between them.

"Um, yeah," Ryo said, rubbing the back of his neck. "I doubt they'd get much sleep tonight, anyway."

"Maybe if we read them bedtime stories." I shot Jhaeros a hopeful look before returning my attention to Ryo. "I hate to interrupt their romantic getaway so soon, but you should probably tell Mel and Lyklor they need to return."

Ryo coughed. The tips of his ears turned pink. "Uh, so I might have tried dreamscaping to them earlier . . . to, you know, wish them luck again."

HOLIDAY CROWN

Jhaeros folded his arms over his chest. Folas grunted.

"Anyway, I appeared at the room number they'd given me to a resort in Dubai, but the suite was empty. Everything inside was pristine—the bed made, towels untouched. There were no bags, only a note on the table." Ryo frowned. "It said, '*Ha-ha. Nice try, Ryo. See ya when we see ya.*'"

"Oh, for pits sake." I groaned into my hands.

"Totally irresponsible," Ryo said as though we were in complete agreement.

Sometimes I had to remind myself that Ryo was no longer my juvenile little brother-in-law but an actual king, and one of my sister's mates. Yeah, I had to remind myself a lot. Same with Mel and Lyklor. The whole lot of them were missing the "responsible older sibling" gene.

Maybe if Ryo had backed off, they wouldn't have felt the need to give him the slip. It was easier being irritated at Ryo than my sister. How were we supposed to contact her in case of an emergency? Granted, nothing noteworthy had occurred for sixteen years, but that was no reason to be lax.

"Ryo, Folas, send Fraya and Lark over and stay with the children while we fill them in."

Both males obeyed immediately, as though I'd resumed my long-ago role as acting queen.

Ryo was in charge . . . but that didn't mean I couldn't boss him and everyone else around. Once a queen, always a queen. No crown necessary.

CHAPTER SIX

Fraya

"Okay, guys, pick out some books to bring with us," I instructed the kids.

Grin lighting her face, Gayla immediately started a stack, which included coloring books and a pack of crayons. When it was about to reach a head tall, Folas walked over and patted her back gently.

"I think you have enough there, Gayla." When she looked up at him with pleading eyes, he smiled. "Maybe just a couple more."

Squealing, Gayla skipped over to a pile of holiday picture books from the mortal world and began sorting through.

"Bleh! Books." Reed wrinkled his nose. "Where are all the toys? Mom would let us play with toys."

"Mom would want you to go to bed and sleep," Lark countered.

My mom and Uncle Ryo had set out to question everyone in the castle, leaving us to help my father and Folas round up the children.

HOLIDAY CROWN

My father grabbed the stack of books Gayla had amassed. "All right, everyone, let's go get comfortable. It's going to be a long night."

I took Gayla's hand. Lark looked as though he had to squeeze tightly to his brothers' fingers to keep the twins from pulling free. They yanked around like a pair of hyper dogs fighting their leashes.

"Reed. Ronin. Stop it," I said.

Usually, they listened to me better, but they were extra wired tonight with all the excitement. Reed yanked free, but not before Folas caught him. Seeing the blond giant escorting Reed down the hall motivated Ronin to behave the remainder of the way.

As we passed grim-faced guards and flaming torches, unease swirled inside my belly. Had news traveled to the stables? Was Alok worried about me? I didn't like the way we'd left things. As soon as it was safe, I'd find a way to speak to him before my parents asked Folas to open a portal home.

My father led us to a suite in the hall where Uncle Ryo had grown up. There was only one door leading in and out. It was nice to get away from the parlor, at least. This suite had adjoining rooms. It looked like a double bed had been moved into the middle chamber.

"If you and Gayla want to get some rest, that one's for you," my dad said.

I thanked him even though I didn't plan on sleeping until Mom and Uncle Ryo caught Malon's accomplice. Hopefully, Gayla would drift off after a story. She handed me a book, then climbed on to the bed. I joined her, sitting on top of the blankets.

"Why don't you get comfortable?" I suggested.

Gayla chewed on her bottom lip a moment before pulling half the covers aside and burrowing in.

"Comfy?" I asked with a smile.

She nodded and looked at the hardcover book in my hands. It was *The Night Before Christmas*.

"Marco," Dad called from the other room.

"Polo," the boys echoed back.

It was another game from the human world Aunt Mel had taught us.

"Marco," Dad said.

"Polo!"

I opened the book to the first page and began reading. "'Twas the night before Christmas, when all through the house not a creature was stirring, not even a mouse.'"

"Marco."

"Polo!" Reed and Ronin shrieked as they raced past on their way to the third connecting room.

"'The stockings were hung by the chimney with care, in hopes that St. Nicholas soon would be there,'" I continued.

"Marco," Dad said, entering our room with a white cravat tied around his eyes.

Gayla and I kept quiet.

"Polo" came the twins' answers from the next room. I swear I heard one gulp. Grinning, Dad headed into the third chamber, calling "Marco" as he went.

"Polo."

"Marco."

"Polo."

"Marco."

"Po—ohhh! Eeeee!" One of the twins squealed right before my dad said a triumphant, "Gotcha!"

Dad and the twins pattered past us. From Reed's pouty face, I'd say he was the one my dad had snatched. Way to go, Pops!

I bent my head over the book, searching for the next line. "'The children were nestled all snug in their beds, while visions of sugarplums danced in their heads.'"

"Fraya? What are sugarplums?"

I squinted at the word, then pursed my lips in thought. "I think it's a type of fruit in the mortal realm."

"Like sweetberries?"

"Yeah, but bigger. Like this," I said, making a fist.

"Oh." Gayla snuggled in closer. "Can you read me every book?"

I glanced at the tall pile on the dresser. Under normal circumstances, this room looked like it was for garments. "Let's see how the night goes," I suggested before picking up where I'd left off. I covered the reindeers, sleigh, rooftop landing, and chimney entrance with toys. By the time jolly St. Nick was filling stockings with toys, Gayla's lashes had fluttered closed.

I kept going, reaching the end. "'Happy Christmas to all, and to all a good night.'" I held still, listening to Gayla's steady breathing. "Gayla?" I whispered.

Soft breaths drifted from her partially open mouth. Smiling to myself, I closed the book soundlessly. I scooted as gently as I could to the edge of the bed and had almost made it off when Gayla's eyes fluttered open.

"What's next?" she asked.

I chuckled and shook my head. So be it. At least the boys were sticking to their room in front and mellowing out from the sounds of it.

"Is it bigger than a breadbox?" I heard Ronin ask.

I slid off the bed and sifted through the books on the dresser. "How about *The Polar Express*?"

"Okay," Gayla said eagerly.

I rejoined her on the bed and began reading, my voice filling our snug room. Like Gayla, I had many questions while reading the odd notions from Earth, but I kept them to myself, answering Gayla as best I could. At some point, she stopped asking questions. The room next door grew quiet as well. Could the males have succeeded in tiring out the twins? I continued reading to the end of the book, not wanting to break the spell of tranquility.

It sounded so quiet without my words filling the room. Surely Dad, Folas, and Lark hadn't drifted off.

When I got off the bed, Gayla did not stir. I set the book with the others and grabbed the bow I'd set beside them. Ever so slowly, I pulled an arrow from the quiver and threaded it as I moved stealthily for the opening between rooms. It was a precautionary measure only. If something had happened, I would have heard a cry of alarm. A scuffle. Something.

When Lark appeared from around the dividing wall, I gave a start and sucked in a breath.

He glanced at my bow and offered a reassuring grin. "The twins finally fell asleep," he whispered, getting close to me and lowering his voice further. "We're keeping quiet to make sure it stays that way. Looks like Gayla is out too." He jutted his chin toward the bed.

"Yeah." I set the bow and arrow gently on top of the books.

"Hey," Lark said, leaning so close our noses practically touched.

Recalling Alok's earlier taunt, I nearly pulled away. He'd spoken in anger. I shouldn't let his words get under my skin, but they'd managed to burrow in and begin to itch with Lark sharing breathing space. Needing to keep quiet, I stood my ground.

"Sorry about earlier. I hope you didn't get into too much trouble."

I relaxed at Lark's apology. He'd acted like the protective brother I didn't have. We'd grown up together, not counting all the time he and his family spent in the mortal realm and Dahlquist. Sometimes we accompanied them, but most of our time together was spent in Pinemist. My parents weren't much for travel beyond my tournaments around the elven realm.

"My dad was mad, but my mom was cool about it," I said.

Lark raised his eyebrows as though surprised. "Aerith wasn't angry?"

"She's a female. I guess she understands what I'm going through." I shrugged. Mom had always treated me like an adult, even when I was a child. Because of this, I'd tried hard not to let her down.

"She didn't care that you were found with a faerie?"

What an odd question. I squinted at Lark. At least he hadn't said "servant." That had been rude and uncalled for, no matter how angry he'd been at the time. "My uncles are faeries."

"But you won't see him again, right?" he pressed.

I stepped back and folded my arms. "Is this really the time to be discussing this?"

"Just answer the question, Fraya."

Something about his tone gave me pause. I narrowed my eyes. "I don't need you looking out for me. I'm a grown female, older than you, and I'll see whomever I please."

Rather than pout or scowl as I'd anticipated, a wide grin spread across Lark's face. "I am so pleased to hear that."

My eyes widened in alarm as Lark lurched forward, clapping one hand over my mouth while pinching my nose with his other. What in the seven hells was happening? I tried to scream. When Lark released my nose, I breathed in deeply, feeling a tickle go up my nostrils, nearly causing me to sneeze. Drowsiness overcame me from out of nowhere. My lids grew weighted. Holding my body up felt like the hardest thing I'd ever had to do. If it weren't for Lark, I would have fallen to the floor.

If it weren't for Lark, I wouldn't be falling asleep as a distant part of my mind begged for consciousness.

CHAPTER SEVEN

Fraya

A mouth awoke me—the firm press of lips on mine. I gave a jerk, my eyes opening to find I was seated on a chair in the attic, Alok standing in front of me with a heated gaze probing my face. A single lantern lit the small space. It might have been romantic if I hadn't been abducted and tied to a chair.

I jerked at the ropes binding my wrists and tried to kick out, but my ankles were secured.

"Sorry about this, Fraya."

I glared at Alok. "Did you glamour yourself to look like Lark?"

"I did." The flame from the lantern glinted off his teeth when he grinned.

"How?" I demanded.

"It is a skill I possess as a Fae royal."

"Fae royal?" I blinked several times.

"A royal prince," he stated proudly, lifting his head. I hated how gorgeous he still looked, despite his wicked betrayal. One hand propped above his hip, Alok's chin lifted higher. "I am Alok Elmray, exiled prince of Ravensburg and son of King Albedo."

My jaw dropped. "Albedo's dead."

"He impregnated my mother before Liri killed him."

No. It wasn't possible, was it? I'd never heard so much as a rumor that Ryo's late brother had sired a child. But Alok couldn't lie. My eyes widened in horror. "But Lulu adopted you."

"My real mother arranged that—not that the simpleton knew any better."

My lips drew back. "You shouldn't talk about your mother that way."

"Lulu was never my mother."

"She raised you. Loved you."

Alok scowled. He stomped over, gripping my chair as he leaned close. I tried to lean back, but there was nowhere to go. Alok laughed. "What about you, Fraya? Did you love me before discovering we were enemies?" His gaze dropped to my lips, reminding me of his kiss moments before as though I'd been Sleeping Beauty and he the prince come to wake and rescue me. Ugh. There was no fairy-tale ending in our future, just bitter disgust.

"Why are we enemies?" I asked. "Aren't we family?"

Alok pushed away from the chair, shaking his head. "We're not family. We have no blood relation, not like you and your cousins. Lark's father betrayed mine. His uncle made my mother a widow before she'd given birth."

My heart twisted into knots tighter than the ones binding my wrists and ankles. "Alok, what have you done with Lark?" Cold dread iced over my skin.

Grinning, Alok walked around me to the back of my chair and spun me around in it. The legs scraped over the attic's dusty floor. Once turned, I saw Lark tied to a chair on the other side of the attic, head slumped to one side.

"Sound asleep and no threat at all," Alok said beside my ear.

"What about my father, Folas, and the twins?" I demanded.

"Sleeping. I only gave you a small pinch of the powder. Everyone else got the full dose. But don't fret, Fraya. I mean none of you harm."

"Then what is it you want?"

"The crown, of course."

"Are you insane? You think you can single-handedly take over Dahlquist and rule over the kingdom?"

Had Alok always been mad? If so, he'd hidden it well. I'd believed him to be the handsome and attentive adopted son of Lulu. I didn't recognize the male who stood in front of me now.

"This isn't for me. It's for my mother. And for the memory of my father. Malon will help us."

"Malon's dead."

Alok smirked. "You mean the guard he glamoured to look like him?"

Overcome by dizziness, I sagged against the back of the chair. Everything in me grew cold as though winter had fallen over the castle. Unlike back home, it was the hot season in Dahlquist. Despite the chills racking my body, there'd be no white Christmas in Dahlquist, no Christmas at all if we didn't stop Malon and Alok. How could I have been so blind? Father was right. I was stupid.

No, not stupid. I'd been tricked. Betrayed. I could berate myself later. Right now, I had to figure out a way to outsmart Alok. Maybe I could use his feelings for me to gain the upper hand.

"That was a clever performance on my uncle's part," Alok continued proudly. "'He's coming! He's got sleeping dust!'" he mocked before chuckling. "The rest of the guards rushed forward to stab the decoy before he could get a word out."

My heart pounded and ears rang. "You got an innocent guard killed." I glared up at him.

I didn't have my mother's calm cool. I couldn't sit quietly listening to Alok's revolting actions. I hated that I'd ever kissed him. I hated sharing breathing space with the duplicitous scoundrel. I'd heard all about his villain of a father and shrew of a mother from Aunt Mel. Apparently the rotten apple didn't fall far from the tree.

Alok clenched his teeth. "It wasn't my intention for anyone to die. Malon was protecting himself. No one else has to get harmed so long as they do as we say."

"You make me sick," I spat.

Anger flashed through Alok's eyes. He stomped up to me. "Lies," he hissed as he gripped the back of my chair and tilted me forward. He crouched down until we were at eye level. His dark brown irises seemed to swirl around his pupils. "You wanted me to be your first, Fraya. Me!"

"I wanted the nice male I knew—Lulu's son, not this monster you've been hiding." My upper lip curled.

Alok stood and set my chair back level with the ground. His shoulders relaxed. "I was always myself with you, Fraya. And you deserve more than a servant's son. You should be with a Fae prince."

I scowled up at him. "Don't you dare tell me you're doing this for me."

Alok's shoulders dropped. He strolled toward Lark, making my heart pound against my rib cage. "As I said, I'm doing it for my mother. That doesn't change the fact that you belong with royalty—a worthy male who isn't related to you by blood." He stopped and stared at Lark then spun around, facing me. "I know all about the past. I know my father first tried to woo your mother and failed miserably. I succeeded where he did not. I made her daughter fall for me."

"Don't flatter yourself," I snarled. "Do you think you're the first boy I've kissed? There have been others . . . back home. You were nothing special."

Alok's eyes sparkled when he grinned. "It must be nice having the ability to lie."

"I despise you, Alok, and that is one hundred percent the truth."

"You're angry," he corrected. "For that, I am sorry. But this is something I must do."

I couldn't even watch him walk away, only listen to his boot steps as they left the attic. As much as I loathed being around him, I didn't want him to leave. My father, Folas, Gayla, and the twins were all incapacitated. My mother and Uncle Ryo thought Malon was no longer a threat.

"Wait!" I cried, yanking at the bindings.

Alok didn't answer. He continued walking toward the stairwell that led back down to the castle. My heart dropped with each footfall that faded away.

"Lark!" I yelled. "Lark!"

My screams were no use. My cousin remained slumped over his chair, not giving the slightest twitch. I needed him to wake the freak up.

My mind reeled. When had Alok gotten to Lark? Had he blown the cursed sleeping dust over him after they'd left the attic? Had he used the disguise to gain entrance into the dungeons before knocking out the guards? I shuddered at how well he'd played the part of my cousin. Alok had the advantage of having grown up at the castle. He'd had years to observe Lark, plenty of occasions to study us all.

I ground my teeth, angry at Alok and mad at myself for being duped.

How long had he been planning this, and why now? Perhaps Aunt Mel's and Uncle Lyklor's absence had presented the best opportunity. Everyone knew King Liri was ruthless. Uncle Ryo, on the other hand, was a kind and caring king. Alok and Malon probably intended to exploit that.

Gritting my teeth, I threw my body weight forward. I managed to scoot the chair forward bit by bit. I didn't know what good it would do reaching Lark, but I made my way across the attic to him, gasping with breath once I reached him. He didn't look comfortable with his head hanging to one side, blond bangs falling over his closed eyelids.

"Lark!"

Nothing. Nope. Yelling directly into his face didn't work either.

Screaming in frustration, I shoved against the ground, sending my chair careening backward. As I tumbled, I curled my chin to my chest to avoid hitting the back of my head on the hard ground. Didn't need to knock myself out.

Wood cracked between the hard floor and my weight. I rolled to one side then back to the other, grinding the chair into the floor. I wiggled my arms and pushed at the ropes circling my wrists until the bindings loosened. I was able to slip my right hand out first. Hissing at the rope burn as it bit at my wrist, I untied my left wrist followed by my ankles. On my feet, I untied Lark then grabbed him under the arms and dragged him to the attic stairs. I couldn't leave my cousin up there unconscious in case Alok returned.

HOLIDAY CROWN

Lark's boots clunked against each stair as I pulled him down, down, down to the corridor flanking the castle ballroom. Guards who had stood earlier against the walls were now strewn across the floor, sleeping. My heart jackhammered.

There wasn't time to take Lark to the suite—Alok knew its location, anyway. So I dragged my cousin into the ballroom and set him gently on the floor beside the doors. If Alok had put him to sleep first, maybe he'd wake up first—hopefully soon.

Closing the ballroom doors behind me, I raced down the hall, heading back to the suite and the bow and arrows I'd left atop the Christmas books on the dresser.

CHAPTER EIGHT

Aerith

"Our scouts have detected no movement in the surrounding fields. No one has tried to leave or enter the castle this eve, Your Highness," the big burly captain of Dahlquist's outer defenses assured Ryo.

I scanned the courtyard for anything suspicious while Ryo finished questioning the captain of the guards.

Mel's entourage, as she called them—Gem, Magnolia, Lulu, and Heath—was helping us out by questioning the servants. If anyone refused to answer, the nearest guards were to escort them down to the dungeon where Ryo would take over the interrogation—that or wait for Mel and Lyklor to return and help. This was one of the few times I wouldn't have minded having Liri around. Feelings aside, this sort of task was his specialty.

"All the outer guards have been accounted for and assembled for your questioning, Your Highness," the captain said.

A line curved around the courtyard walls.

Inwardly, I groaned. I couldn't imagine the accomplice waiting patiently for Ryo's questions. The culprit could be hiding in any number of places inside the castle. But we had to start somewhere, and it made the most sense that this individual had headed to the stables to make his or her getaway the moment Malon was brought down.

"Thank you, Gnax. Keep your eyes and ears open," Ryo said to the captain.

We walked side by side to the start of the line. Before reaching the first guard, I pressed my hand over Ryo's shoulder, stopping him. He turned a questioning gaze to me.

"Should we bring Liri over to help?"

Ryo grimaced before blowing out a breathy sigh. "I suppose he'd be useful."

"He better be. He's the reason we're in this mess," I grumbled.

Ryo nodded, frowning. "I can open a portal, but I can't risk going through. Everything should be fine now, but if I weren't able to make the return trip . . ." He let his sentence hang in the night. Finishing wasn't necessary. If Ryo somehow got stuck in the mortal realm, the castle would be left without a king. Teryani had learned that lesson the hard way.

"I can't go through either." No risk, no matter how minor, was worth being separated from my family. "We'll have to send a trusted guard. Someone nearby," I added.

Not wasting another second, Ryo strode to the line, looking over the guards as he walked swiftly past the watchful faces. He came to a stop in front of a tall, lean guard with brown hair bound in a long ponytail. "Kral, please join me and my sister-and-law for a moment." The guard followed Ryo as he clipped back to me, jaw set. "Kral was one of the guards who accompanied Mel and me to Pinemist and helped defeat the ogres way back when."

Way back when? Ha. I didn't feel like we were that old, but yeah, back in the days before anyone of us were mated parents.

"Thanks for your service," I told Kral.

He nodded. "It was my pleasure to help set things right."

Ryo cleared his throat. "I'm sorry to have to do this, but I need you to tell me you had nothing to do with Malon's escape."

Kral didn't so much as blink. "I had no part in Malon's escape, nor do I know anything leading up to or following the event. It is an honor to serve the kings of Dahlquist—you, my liege; King Lyklor; and King Liri. I would serve no other."

Ryo nodded. "Thank you for your loyal service, Kral. Now I need to send you to the mortal realm to tell Liri what has happened. Tell him we need his immediate help."

"It is my honor," Kral answered.

"Come. I will open a portal."

Kral waited to follow us as Ryo led the way to the nearest portal access point behind the stable. I stood to the side and watched as Ryo opened his arms. He frowned and lowered them.

"What's the matter?" I asked.

Ryo's frown cut grooves along his chin. "I cannot open a portal."

"But that would mean . . ." My heart nearly stopped.

Ryo's hand went to the hilt of the sword tethered to his hip. "Malon isn't dead."

Boots pounded behind us as Ryo led an army of two dozen guards to the throne room doors. Three of the sentinels were females, all armed with swords. I wanted to run straight back to the suites to warn Jhaeros and Folas, but Ryo insisted we'd find Malon in the throne room.

He stopped in front of the large doors and waited as two guards threw them open. Six more of Ryo's sentinels ran into the throne room first.

"Your Majesty, he's here . . . on the dais!" one of the males yelled.

Heart pounding against my chest, I followed Ryo in with the rest of the guards.

Malon said nothing as we stormed in. He sat slouched on the throne, looking as sickly as his glamour had. Without so much as a weapon, he didn't appear to be any threat, but just the fact that he was loose from his cage was enough to put my senses on full alert.

I scanned every dark corner of the room. Too much blood had already been spilled in here when Albedo tried to take the crown. Chills wafted over me, goose bumps rising on my arms. I nocked an arrow in my bow and held it up, trained on Malon, ready to let it loose if he tried anything.

"Hello, Brother," Malon said evenly, as though too tired to muster a sneer.

Blade at his side, Ryo stopped several paces from the dais. "Who let you out?"

Malon chuckled, which led to coughing. Once he got hold of himself, he grinned through the gloom. "You'll find out soon enough."

"Indeed, I will," Ryo said, puffing out his chest. "You can wait in your cell while we track down your accomplice."

"I'm staying right here." Steel entered Malon's voice, sending an icy wave of uncertainty crashing over me.

Ryo laughed. "How do you figure that? You have no weapon, and you're outnumbered. I doubt you could fight a toddler in your condition."

Malon's teeth gleamed when he smiled. "I don't need a weapon. I have your son, Lark, and your niece." He looked briefly in my direction before returning to Ryo.

I had to hold back a scream. Not Fraya! Not my baby girl.

Malon leaned forward, his cruel gaze shooting down at Ryo. "If anything happens to me, my accomplice will stick a dagger in Lark's heart. Then again, maybe you don't care. I hear the golden prince isn't even yours. Sharing a female—an elf—you really are a lost cause, *Brother*." This time Malon did manage to sneer.

Taking a step forward, Ryo snarled up at the blackguard. "What is it you want?"

HOLIDAY CROWN

Malon leapt to his feet, giving us all a start. "I want my brother Albedo back, you cretin! Dahlquist was his birthright. Since he's no longer alive to claim his rightful title, I will ensure that his son does."

All mouths gaped open.

"Son? What son? Albedo wasn't mated long enough to father a child," Ryo said.

Malon grinned. "He was virile enough to impregnate his mate with twins in one night."

Albedo's widow had twins? Pitberries! What were the odds? Only an Elmray could cause this much aggravation. I backed away slowly while Malon's focus remained on Ryo.

"Take off your crown, and set it at my feet," he instructed.

"And after?" Ryo demanded.

"Then you are dismissed to locate a faerie with the authority to crown my nephew. You will bring in all of the castle's captains and servant heads to bear witness. Afterward, I will release you from the castle. Once you are through the gates and across the drawbridge, I will send your son and niece out safely. Do as I ask, and this I promise: No harm will come to you or your family."

"And I'm supposed to believe this?" Ryo demanded.

With a smile, Malon stuck out his tongue then retracted it. "I am not a liar like Lyklor. You have your nephew to thank. If it were up to me, I would hunt you all down one by one and slit your throats."

My fist tightened on my bow. Who was this mysterious Elmray heir, and how had he gotten into the castle? Given the date of conception, he'd be nearly the exact same age as Lark—still a boy. It was a wonder Malon chose to obey a fifteen-year-old he'd only just met. Then again, he looked weak from years of neglect. The smug smile on his lips communicated his belief that he would soon regain his strength after running us out of the castle.

Not happening!

As Ryo removed the crown from his head and started slowly toward the dais, I turned on my heel and headed out of the throne room. I had to find Fraya and Lark before Malon's nephew was crowned. The search required swift care. We had no idea who this boy was.

As I ran out of the throne room into the corridor, I was hit by more questions. Why had Malon taken Lark and Fraya but not the twins? Having all of the children would have given him an even stronger hand. I could only come up with one of two conclusions: Either Reed and Ronin had gotten away, or Fraya and Lark had set out on their own and been captured. But Jhaeros would have never allowed the teens to venture out. He wouldn't have let anyone take them, either, not without a fight.

Heart racing, I ran for the suite we were meant to meet up in later.

The guards stationed along the walls leading to the throne room gave me wary glances but kept to their posts. They weren't mine to command. There was nothing they could do to help, anyway.

Skidding to a stop, I faced the nearest guard and asked, "Did you see Fraya or Lark come this way in the last hour?"

"I did not, Lady Keasandoral."

Yep, utterly no use at all.

I pushed forward, bow clutched in one hand, the arrow in the other. I had a full quiver on my back, but I felt better with an arrow in hand—even one I couldn't fire at Malon. Not yet. What about the nephew? A boy? No doubt he'd been brainwashed by his mother. I'd never met Oreal, but Mel had given me an earful. The horrid female had slapped my sister. I owed her one. As for the female's twins . . . I shuddered to think what kind of monsters she and Albedo had created. From the way Malon had spoken, it sounded like only one of Albedo's twins was at the castle aiding him. The other must be a backup.

I rounded the bend, stopping only to ask a guard if he'd seen the kids in this corridor. The answer was another "no."

"Lady Keasandoral!" a young male yelled.

I spun around so quickly my hair lifted off my back.

Alok pumped his arms, gasping for breath when he reached me. He lowered his voice for only my ears. "Fraya and Lark have been taken." His eyes seemed to grab hold of mine and beg for help.

"Did you see where?"

He nodded vigorously. "The kidnapper headed to the royal wing."

Pitberries! It was as though I had instincts into the future. Something had told me that would be a place to look.

"Let's go," I said, already moving swiftly back the way I'd just come.

"Should we get help from the guards?" Alok asked uncertainly, darting a glance from side to side.

"No." I dropped my voice. "We have to keep this quiet until Fraya and Lark are safe." If Malon's nephew was keeping his eyes out, he'd take one look at the group of guards following us and know his hiding spot had been compromised. He'd promised not to hurt our family if we did as he asked. A rescue attempt wasn't part of that bargain. If he saw us coming, he might panic and do something to my daughter or Lark.

Alok nodded in understanding, keeping his voice down. "I heard what was happening and went to check on Fraya." Warm affection laced his words.

Now probably wasn't the right time to tell Alok that after I found Fraya it was a safe bet we wouldn't be visiting Faerie again anytime soon. I'd always preferred family time in Pinemist. This latest attack at Dahlquist was another strike against leaving the safety of our own realm.

The guards watched in silence as we passed. They were probably wondering why the freak berries I'd been running frantically one moment and now glided by the way I'd come, appearing relatively calm. Inside, I felt like my heart was a spinning top, making my head feel dizzy.

Luckily, Ryo didn't walk out of the throne room as we passed. I needed him to do as Malon said so the elusive heir would believe he was getting his spoiled rotten way. I couldn't believe we were being played by a fifteen-year-old. I wouldn't make the mistake of underestimating him. He'd abducted my daughter and Lark. It was my job to ensure it was the shortest kidnapping in the history of Faerie.

Outside the royal wing, we found the guards slumped over the ground, sleeping. I nocked my arrow in my bow and nodded at the door leading into the open hall. Alok acknowledged my nod with one of his own and carefully opened the door. Together, we slid into the hall, night air wafting warmly over our faces. Alok didn't have a weapon, so he followed me, inching up until he was walking at my side. In the moonlight, the blue strands in his hair shone against the black. It was a striking combination, much better than Lulu's first attempt. She probably wouldn't be thrilled if she knew he was creeping up on a deranged Elmray heir with me. I still remembered her excitement the first time she introduced me to him. Alok was seven at the time. He'd been abandoned by his birth mother at the Fable Festival. Lulu had found him crying beside a food cart. Once it was clear no one was coming to claim the boy, Lulu had brought him back to the castle and adopted him. I hadn't paid him much attention over the years.

When had he and my daughter formed an attachment?

Without hesitation, Alok stepped forward and opened the door leading into the inner halls of the sumptuous royal wing. Several steps later, he was leading the way. He looked sure-footed. Unafraid.

Dread coiled around my throat and descended into my belly as I stared at the back of his dark head of hair. "Alok, do you remember your birth mother's name?"

"She never told me. It was just 'Mom.'" He didn't lower his tone as he had around the guards stationed along the throne room corridors.

We were alone in the royal wing. He'd led me here, and I'd blindly followed. I lifted my bow and arrow, aiming the tip at the back of his skull. Alarm turned into a sick punch to the gut. I didn't know if I had it in me to shoot a boy in the back of the head. I lowered the arrow slowly down his neck, past his shoulder blades, stopping at his hip. I could wound him though. First, I had to be certain.

"Are you Albedo Elmray's son?"

I stopped, arrow aimed as Alok turned around. My breath hitched in the microsecond I waited to see the expression on his face. Hand lifted to his lip, Alok blew shimmery dust at me. I released my arrow, but blindsided, it hit the stone floor rather than flesh.

It was as though a tidal wave had washed over me. My shoulders and arms drooped. The bow was sucked down to the ground by an invisible undertow.

"I apologize for this, Lady Keasandoral. Rest assured I mean you and your family no harm. I am merely righting a wrong."

"Don't do this," I managed to say before dropping to the ground like a sack of grains.

CHAPTER NINE

Fraya

The guards in the halls leading to Uncle Ryo's old suites were all knocked out, slumped into green-and-gold heaps on the ground. At least they had been put to sleep rather than slaughtered. Alok wasn't pure evil. Ugh. I still wanted to scrub my lips and burn my bodysuit.

Back in the suite, I found my father and everyone else safe and asleep. I snatched my bow and quiver from the adjoining room, careful not to wake Gayla, whose chest rose and fell gently on the bed. My gaze paused on her, a sense of responsibility washing over me. I needed to help protect the children.

With careful footsteps, I left the suite and set out in search of my mother and Uncle Ryo. It wasn't too difficult to figure out the route Alok had taken—just follow the trail of unconscious bodies.

They started toward the throne room then veered off down a corridor adjacent.

When the halls filled with muffled voices and footsteps, I retraced my steps and peeked around the corner. Seeing the twin's nannies, Kaylin and Peridot, heading to the throne room's main doors, I sprinted over to them. The females wore loose day dresses and cloaks that looked as though they had been pulled on hastily.

"Fraya," Peridot said, eyes lighting up.

"Do you know what's happening?" My words rushed out of my lips.

Peridot shook her head. "We were summoned by guards from our chambers to come to the throne room by order of King Ryo. Do you know what this is about?"

My frown tightened. What was happening? What was Alok's plan? "I don't know," I said, even though I had some idea. There wasn't time to explain.

"We need to get in there," Kaylin said.

"Before you go, can I borrow your cloak?"

"Of course, Miss Fraya." Peridot spoke first. She pulled off her forest green cloak and handed it to me without question. My aunt and uncles had the nicest staff.

"Thank you," I said, clutching the fabric with my bow.

As Kaylin and Peridot headed into the throne room, I raced around the corner to the next hall, where I set my bow against the wall while putting on Peridot's cloak. Glamour wasn't one of my abilities, so I'd have to try for a disguise. I pulled the hood low over my head, picked up the bow, and selected two arrows from the quiver. I wouldn't need extras. I never missed. The arrows I stuffed into one of the cloak's voluminous sleeves. The bow I pressed with my elbow against my side, hidden by the draping fabric. Taking a deep breath,

HOLIDAY CROWN

I rounded the corner with purposeful strides toward the throne room.

Time to put an end to Alok's attempt at the crown. He'd released a dangerous villain and put my entire family at risk for some petty vendetta. He had no business ruling over Dahlquist. I couldn't wait to best the bastard. I looked forward to watching the look of dismay in his eyes when I shot him with my arrow. Did he really think he could kiss me, deceive me, make me feel things for him, then tie me up in the attic and get away with it?

I'd shoot an arrow through his heart for toying with mine.

Ahead of me, a broad-shouldered guard with a fancy clasp around his waist walked through the open doors of the throne room. I slipped in right behind him, using his burly physique as a wall. I followed in his footsteps, up to the dais where roughly fifteen servants had gathered. Uncle Ryo stood in front of them, his arms folded, facing the sallow figure in front of the throne. I presumed the sickly black-haired male was Malon. My stomach lurched when I saw Uncle Ryo's crown in his pale fingers—fingers that plucked the pieces of greenery off and threw them on the ground until the crown was picked clean of its festive embellishments.

I didn't look for long, keeping to the guard's shadow as close as I could without raising suspicion. I stood angled out of eyesight from Kaylin and Peridot. I didn't want them to recognize me in the cloak I'd just borrowed and wave me over or call my name. My heartbeat was all over the place, and I had to keep my arm with the arrows raised enough to prevent my weapons from slipping out of the sleeve.

A tall skinny guard held a torch beside the assembled group, casting light where the darkened windows above did not. A quick scan of the crowd made my heart drop. Alok wasn't here. Neither was my mother. Where had she gone?

An elderly male with cropped gray hair was called forward.

"This is Mural. He can perform the ceremony," Ryo said with bitter disgust.

Malon's grin made the contents of my stomach turn to ash.

"Very good, Brother. Shall I make the announcement, or do you want to address your gathered subjects . . . one last time?"

Uncle Ryo turned and faced the group with a grim frown. "Malon and his nephew have kidnapped my son and niece. I must hand over the crown in order to save them. I apologize for this disruption in leadership, but no kingdom is worth the price of my family. My hand might be forced tonight, but I promise you this doesn't end here."

Malon snarled. "I should cut out your son's tongue for your insolence."

A dark shadow fell over Uncle Ryo's face as he turned. "Touch one hair on my son's head, and I won't just keep you alive; I'll make sure every second is agony and that your torture lasts for an eternity." I'd never heard my uncle speak with such cruel conviction. In this case, I was encouraged by his sense of vengeance. If only he knew he didn't have to worry about Lark or me.

I craned my head, desperate to spot Alok. I wanted both blackguards in my sights. He must be awaiting his ill-gotten crown in the antechamber beside the dais. Coward.

"Enough threats," Malon snapped. "It is time to crown the rightful king of Dahlquist, Albedo's son, our nephew. King Alok Elmray."

"Alok?" Uncle Ryo choked.

Just wait until Mom and Dad found out. They'd be gagging too.

The guard in front of me shifted to the left. I shuffled the same way, keeping my head bent but eyes alert.

"Send your officiator up to the dais," Malon commanded.

Uncle Ryo must have given the elderly male a look of consent because the frail faerie shuffled forward.

"And you, Brother, you will do the honors of placing the crown on our nephew's head."

Gritting his teeth, Uncle Ryo made his way up the dais. With a nasty smirk, Malon held the golden crown out to him. Uncle Ryo clutched it in his hand.

"You there, with the torch, stand up here with us, but not too close. I have not seen much light in over a decade." Malon's bitter laughter crawled over the stone walls enclosing the throne room.

After the skinny guard stepped out of the crowd, the guards and staff moved forward as though following the light his torch cast. I wasn't expecting the wall of muscle in front of me to move so quickly, leaving me with only the cover of the cloak. Naturally, that was when Peridot noticed me from the cluster of castle staff she stood with. The confusion wrinkling her forehead smoothed out as she smiled at the sight of me. I thought I saw her lips moving. Heart jackhammering, I hurried forward as though I could blend back in with the guards. Hopefully she would comprehend my wish to remain hidden. In my haste, the bow slipped from my elbow.

Horror washed over me when I felt it leave my side and clatter to the floor. The guards in front of me turned to look. I pulled back my hood and yelled, "Uncle Ryo, stop! Lark and I are safe."

Not wasting a second, Uncle Ryo bellowed, "Guards, seize him!"

I dove for my bow and shook an arrow free from my sleeve. As I straightened, the skinny guard on the dais threw his torch to the ground. A crackling wall of fire flamed up, cutting us off from the throne. It burned from one wall to the other, forming a deliberate barrier. Uncle Ryo was trapped with Malon and the guard who had to be Alok, glamoured again.

I bellowed in frustration. The elderly faerie would be no help to Uncle Ryo at all. But I could still shoot through fire. Flinging off the cloak, I strode forward as close as I dared without getting singed. Behind the flames, Malon and Alok closed in on Uncle Ryo and started pulling, pushing, and twisting around in one dark mass.

My heart rate was all over the place. I tried to steady my breath as I lifted my arrow and watched for an opening. Even with two against one, Uncle Ryo was able to fling off Malon. The gangling Fae seemed to roll away and disappear off the back end of the dais.

Pitberries!

Well, he wouldn't be able to hide for long. Alok was the mastermind behind this whole terrible affair. He was the one to beat.

As though sensing my mind on him, his glamour morphed into the handsome boy with whom I'd shared too many kisses and exploratory touches.

Uncle Ryo's mouth gaped open, still looking shocked by the truth. Alok took advantage of his surprise and whipped out a small crimson pouch.

"No!" I yelled, letting an arrow loose in an attempt to stop Alok as he flung the contents of the velvet pouch into my uncle's wide-eyed face.

My arrow found Alok's arm, piercing his flesh. He gave a cry of pained surprise as the shaft protruded from his limb. But it was too late. Uncle Ryo fell with a heavy thud onto the dais. Alok had already sprinted for the antechamber with unnatural speed before I could aim my second arrow.

As the flames crept toward the wood dais, my heart shot up my throat. Uncle Ryo would burn to death if we didn't get him out of there.

Several guards were already running to the chamber doors. They could access the dais from the antechamber. By the time they reached it, Malon and Alok would have escaped.

I fidgeted in place, my fingers twitching and mind speeding faster than my heart. I waited until a guard ran through the antechamber and pulled Uncle Ryo to safety before spinning on my heel and running out of the throne room.

My ears were met with shouting, guards banding into groups to hunt down Alok and Malon. I looked to the right and left, trying to decide which way to go. The castle's halls were like a labyrinth. I knew which direction the males would have first emerged from, fleeing the dais, but that hall also connected to more leading to the family suites. They wouldn't have to fight their way past the main doors to reach the area of the castle where Alok had already incapacitated guards.

Father! My mind screeched. I took off running, yelling at nearby guards to join me. Our boots pounded the flagstones. It felt like I'd entered an alternative universe or had slipped into a really trippy dream. Where was my mom? She and I were the only family members left conscious . . . unless Alok had gotten to her too.

A cold shiver ran over my balmy skin. I might be the only one left to defend the royal family against Malon and Alok. Well, me and the guards charging down the hall at my back. Captain Fraya to the rescue!

HOLIDAY CROWN

I led the castle guards straight to the suite, where I was relieved to find everyone all accounted for and still sleeping.

The guards did a quick search of the room with me. One cleared his throat before approaching me. "Miss Fraya, I found this on the bed."

My fingers shook as I took the note from him. Hastily scrawled words in red crayon were made out to me.

Fraya,

If you want your mother to remain safe, come to the royal suites alone.

Everything went cold around me. It was as though my veins had turned to ice. One wrong move and they'd shatter inside me. There would be no warmth in any world without my mom. I knew exactly how Uncle Ryo felt handing over his crown to save his family.

No price was too high when it came to my parents. Alok could have the golden crown and pretend to be king all he wanted so long as he let the rest of us go.

I should have aimed for his black heart.

CHAPTER TEN

Fraya

I was on my own without counsel or aid.

I'd ordered the guards to stay and watch over my family in the suite. The moment my father or Folas woke, they were to tell them what had transpired. I couldn't count on either of the adults to come around in time. It was now up to me to negotiate.

Each step led me closer to the royal wing. The flagstones felt rough and cold beneath my booted soles. The flames sputtered and hissed from the torches as I breezed by.

I had one purpose: to save my family.

Alok and Malon stood in the hall outside the king and queen's chamber. Well, Alok stood. Malon must have dragged a chair from one of the rooms. He slouched into a plum velvet wingback chair with Alok standing beside him. Seeing Uncle Ryo's crown atop Alok's head made me want to shoot Alok where he stood. Only concern for my mother stayed my hand. The earlier wound I'd inflicted wasn't to be seen beneath an embroidered midnight jacket he must have stolen from Liri's wardrobe. Thieving Fae making himself at home and wearing the crown without any kind of coronation.

Again, I wondered how he'd fooled me so thoroughly.

"Put down the bow, Fraya." The look in Alok's eyes was grave. He frowned and spoke without his earlier affection. Good. Perhaps my arrow had affectively communicated my newfound loathing for him.

"I want to see my mother first."

Alok opened the door to Liri's chamber. "You may look from the hallway," he said.

I clipped over, stopping when I had a clear view inside the chamber. My mother lay motionless on her back atop the bed. With a cry of alarm, I tried to rush in, only to be blocked by Alok.

"You have to give me your bow and arrow."

I shoved the bow and arrow at Alok then rammed past him, throwing in an elbow for good measure. Hurrying to the bedside, relief filled me when I noticed the gentle rise and fall of Mom's chest.

"I would never hurt her," Alok said defensively.

"That's not what your note said." I whipped around and glared at him.

Alok's face darkened. "I instructed you not to bring guards so she wouldn't be harmed in any crossfire. Aerith always treated me kindly. Plus, she's your mother. I mean it when I say I would never hurt her."

"No. You'd just knock her out and threaten her entire family," I said. "What would have happened if my uncle refused to hand over his crown?" I sneered up at his head. "Would you have made good on your threat to kill Lark and me?"

"You—never."

"What about Lark?" I yelled, fury surging through my veins and burning up my earlier chills.

Malon slunk into the room with a jeering grin and leaned against the wall. I felt revolted by the creepy look he cast over us. "What is this? A lover's quarrel or a siege? Get on with the negotiations, Nephew."

Alok lifted his nose and looked down at Malon. "Do not forget I freed you. I am in charge. I am king."

"That crown doesn't make you king," I spat.

Alok turned his head to me. His movements were deliberate, careful, not used to the weight of a crown. "You're right," he said. "Once Ryo awakens, I need him to oversee my coronation. For that, he will need proper motivation. It would be easier for you to carry one of the twins to me. I'll let you decide whether to bring me Reed or Ronin. Afterward, we will deposit Aerith at the outer doors of the royal wing. You can arrange for guards to help carry your family to a carriage and leave the castle. Once I am crowned, Ryo and his son will be allowed to leave as well."

It wasn't his inability to lie so much as the sincerity of his tone that caused a deep ache to enter my chest. Alok had made his choice. Whether or not he wanted us safe didn't change the fact that he'd gone against my family. The scoundrel thought he could kick my uncles and cousins out of their rightful home. I could only imagine what Liri would do to Alok. Would he cut open his throat as he had Alok's father? I'd made Mom tell me all the family history, especially the bits she'd been part of. Did Alok know my mom had witnessed his father's death?

I glanced at her sleeping form on the bed, watching her for several heartbeats before returning my attention to Alok. "You know Liri won't let you get away with this, right?"

"As long as Malon remains at Dahlquist, the portal access points will remain dormant." There wasn't a trace of concern in Alok's tone.

Liri could still portal to Faerie and try to sneak in through the gates, though I imagined Alok would keep a sharp eye on who came and went.

"I'm sorry, Fraya, but it is time for you to get one of your cousins and bring him back to me. Do not bring anyone else with you."

"Or what? You'll hurt my mother?" I put my hands on my hips. I wanted to force the bastard to say the words. Break his promise the way he'd destroyed my trust.

"He won't, but I will." Malon detached himself from the wall and prowled toward the bedside, but not before I got between the sickly bastard and my mother.

"Stay away from her," I snarled.

Malon's cracked lips curled over yellowed teeth. "You're lucky my nephew wants between your legs, pet, otherwise we wouldn't be having this conversation."

"Do not speak to her that way," Alok snapped.

Malon scoffed and shook his head. "Never get involved with an elf, Nephew. It always ends badly."

"It didn't for Ryo or Lyklor," Alok argued.

Malon laughed cruelly. "They're sharing a crown and a female. They might as well cut off their balls while they're at it. Like I said, it always ends badly." His yellowed teeth grinned manically.

I walked several steps toward Alok. "Do you really expect me to leave my mother while he's here?" I demanded.

The dark pretender winced beneath his stolen crown. Alok's eyes stuck to mine like he was probing for something. Irises the darkest brown seared me. He seemed frozen, his chest barely rising as though he didn't breathe. My heart, on the other hand, was all over the place. If he cared about me at all, he wouldn't allow Malon anywhere near my mother.

"Make him leave the room first," I said. I'd been prepared to plead with Alok if that's what it took, but the voice that rose out of me now came out as a command.

Dark gaze still on me, Alok's shoulders began to relax. I could see him beginning to relent when Malon snarled and lunged for me, dagger in hand. I blinked, wondering if I'd imagined the weapon. It was as though it had appeared from thin air. Bony fingers grabbed me around the waist and held the blade at my throat.

"Let her go!" Alok yelled.

Ignoring him, Malon hissed in my ear. "You don't give the orders, Elf!"

HOLIDAY CROWN

Alok took a step toward us then halted when Malon pressed the blade to my skin. Alok's nostrils flared, fury sparking in his eyes. While the two males faced off, I stomped on Malon's foot. He gasped and jerked, nicking me with his blade. I pushed his arm away and flung myself out of his grip.

Spinning around, I saw Lark crawl out from beneath the bed and rise from the floor, holding a sword. My cousin rushed Malon and shoved his blade all the way through the horrid Fae with a magnificent bellow. The tip of the sword burst through Malon's chest, dripping blood.

Malon's scream died with him. His head slumped forward. With unnatural strength, Lark held him skewered to his sword. My cousin's cheeks blazed red, and fire seemed to dance in his eyes. He looked like a deity sent down by Sky Mother to vanquish our enemies.

I stared in awe.

Alok took one last look at us before making a run for it.

"He's getting away!" I cried as Alok zipped out the door.

Lark blinked several times, seeming to come out of a trance. Malon crashed to the floor, along with Lark's sword. While my cousin put a booted foot to Malon's back and pulled out his sword, I raced after Alok.

Ahead of me, in the hall, he ran with my bow and arrow in one hand while his other held the crown to his head.

I sprinted forward, fueled by rage and adrenaline.

Alok ripped open the door to the corridor. It closed behind him, forcing me to slow down and open it. Starlight seemed to shiver over the surface of the lake below. Moonlight touched the blue streaks in Alok's raven hair.

At the end of the corridor, the air rippled into a circle that widened with each pound of my boots on the flagstones. My heart lurched up my neck. Malon was dead. Alok could open a portal and escape.

Jetting across the dark, open hall, I pushed myself to my limit, no air left in my lungs when I reached for Alok, grasping hold of his arm. He was already slipping through the portal. I had to let go or risk being sucked away with him. It was too late to stop him, but at the last second, I was able to snatch Uncle Ryo's crown from his head.

As Alok disappeared and the portal spun closed, I was left standing in the moonlight, gripping the golden crown.

Footsteps ran out to join me.

"Fraya, are you okay?" Lark called frantically before reaching my side.

I turned slowly, looking at my cousin holding his bloody sword and at my shaking hands gripping the crown.

"I'm fine," I said, steadying my breath. "You woke up." I could have jumped for joy when I saw him in the royal bedchamber. Everything had happened too quickly to process until now. My mind reeled. My heart thundered from the stress of it all. Part of me wanted to collapse against the wall and weep tears of relief.

Lark pressed his free hand to his forehead. "Alok blindsided me after I left the attic. He blew some kind of powder at me, and I fell asleep in an instant. I woke up in the ballroom and started looking around. I had a feeling the fool might check out the royal suite since he confessed who he was and his intentions to become the king of Dahlquist before knocking me out." Lark sneered at the spot where Alok had portaled. "The guards stationed around the south wing were all asleep, so I figured I'd been correct. I snuck in, expecting to confront Alok. But the hall was deserted. I found Aunt Aerith on the bed. I was just deciding on a plan when I heard voices in the hall. I hid under the bed and overheard Alok tell Malon he was waiting for you. So, I waited too."

"Thank goodness you were there," I said, carefully avoiding Lark's sword as I gave him a hug.

When we separated, Lark frowned. "Is everyone else okay?"

"Asleep, but fine," I said.

Working out the timeline together, we figured Lark had been knocked out several hours before everyone else. That meant we still had a little while to wait before the rest of our family woke up. We used the time to inform the castle staff and standing guards of what had transpired. Kaylin and Peridot exclaimed their relief. Everyone bowed when my cousin spoke. I supposed that until Uncle Ryo woke up, Lark was acting king.

"Want this?" I asked, holding up the crown.

Lark drew his lips back as though I'd just offered him a mud pie and suggested he feast upon it. "Pass," he said. "It's hard enough being a prince."

Smiling my understanding, I handed the crown to Peridot and asked her to put it with Uncle Ryo in the throne room's antechamber where we'd been told Dahlquist's true holiday king had been laid over a settee to sleep off the effects of the faerie dust.

I didn't know if Alok had knocked out my mother or father first, so Lark and I split up. We didn't want anyone to wake up and go into a panic. Lark stayed with his brothers, my father, Folas, and Gayla while I sat on the bed beside my sleeping mother. First, I had a couple guards remove Malon's body and the bloodstained rug from the chamber.

Then I waited.

The joy that jolted through me when my mother stirred was like no other.

Parents worried about their children, sure. But kids worried too. My family meant more to me than all the worlds.

Lashes fluttered over blue eyes. My mom jerked up, grasping at the covers.

"Everything's fine now," I said before throwing my arms around her.

"Oh, dear, dear, dear," Lulu said, pacing the parlor where we'd all gathered after everyone was awake. "I had no idea who he really was. I am so sorry." She hugged her arms around her middle, her lower lip trembling.

Magnolia went to her side and rubbed her back while murmuring gentle words for only Lulu's ears.

I felt bad for Lulu. She'd given Alok her love and trust. It wasn't her fault she'd been tricked.

My stomach tightened. In the hours of silence, waiting for my mother to wake, I'd had too much time to replay past kisses and shared affections between Alok and me. Nothing could have prepared me for his betrayal. He'd hidden his intentions well, made me believe that we had something special.

I hated him, and yet it still hurt.

For once, the twins were subdued, watching and listening to everyone around them. They sat side by side on the sofa with Peridot and Kaylin fussing over them. Being coddled was clearly one step too much, because soon they were squirming away from their childhood nannies.

"You did well, Son," Uncle Ryo said proudly. "You and Fraya."

Lark shrugged, but there was no hiding his pleased grin.

My mother inched in closer to me, offering a warm smile. "Are you sure you're okay?" she asked softly.

"Fine," I answered on cue, glad I wasn't forced to tell the truth all the time the way Fae were. "Just exhausted."

Mom nodded. "We can return home or remain here until Mel and Lyklor return."

"Don't leave us!" Ronin yelped, leaping onto the sofa. The little scamp climbed up the back and jumped over. Reed, naturally, followed his lead. Running toward us, they hollered, "Aunt Aerith! Uncle Jhaeros! Don't leave us! Don't leave us!"

"Boys, pipe down!" Uncle Ryo snapped in a rare show of sharp discipline.

The twins stopped in their tracks and shared matching frowns with quivering chins. Ronin's tears seemed to jump over to Reed and catch in his eyes.

I looked at Mom and raised my brows. With a sigh, she crouched to the ground and said, "Of course we'll stay." Smiles lighting up their faces, the twins ran to her and held still long enough for her to hug them.

"That still means going back to bed," Uncle Ryo said sternly.

"But, Dad . . ." Reed began before Uncle Ryo's glare cut him off.

"Can we sleep with Lark?" Ronin asked.

"It's okay with me," Lark said.

"Can I sleep with Fraya?" Gayla asked her dad.

Folas hadn't said much since waking. From the clench of his jaw, you'd think the castle was still under siege. "You're sleeping in my room tonight," he said.

Unlike the twins, Gayla didn't attempt to argue.

Sidling up to me, my mom whispered, "Would you like to share a room with your father and me, just for tonight?"

I screwed up my face. Ugh. Not a chance. "Mom," I groaned.

She smiled. "Or we could stay up and play a game of campaigne."

"All I want is a bath followed by bed."

Gem perked up at that. "We can draw you a bath, Miss Fraya."

"I can manage it myself, thanks," I said quickly. The trouble with having castle staff prepare baths was I never knew if they'd try to enter the water with me and scrub me down.

"Well, at least we're right across the hall if you need us," Mom said.

We walked to our chambers in Cirrus's old wing of the castle. Liri had insisted Mom have it for her visits. She'd had all the rooms redecorated with colorful artwork and comfy furniture. There was always a fuzzy blanket and plump pillows to sink into. Apparently, the hall had once been lined with mirrors. Now a unicorn mural graced a large portion of the wall in the corridor. Mom loved her unicorns.

Outside my door, Father gave me a hug then stepped back as suddenly as he'd dove in. "We love you, Fraya."

I blinked several times, feeling undeserving of his embrace.

"You couldn't have known who Alok really was," Dad said gently. "Lulu never suspected a thing, and she raised him."

"I feel bad for her," I said, not wanting to linger on my feelings.

Dad sighed. "I do too. At least she has close friends at the castle to comfort her. If you need anyone to talk to, you know you can come to us."

I nodded. "Thanks, Dad," I said, even though I had no desire to take him up on his offer. He was just being nice, and I was relieved he didn't bring up my earlier transgression.

After giving my mom a kiss and hug and waving to my parents as they watched me enter my room across from theirs, I found a young female servant filling up the tub with warm water in the attached bathing chamber.

"Gem sent me to fill your tub, Miss Fraya."

"Thanks." Gee, I hoped Gem hadn't woken the poor girl from sleep.

I was too grateful for a rinse to worry overmuch. Once the tub was filled with enough water, I sent the servant back to bed.

Pulling off my leather cuffs, tunic, and bodysuit, I imagined a snake shedding her skin. I shucked it all to the floor before stepping into the tub already scented with jasmine bubbles. Before sinking down into the warm depths, I twisted my hair into a high bun above my head to keep it dry. Grabbing a loofah from the ledge, I gave my body a thorough scrubbing, dabbing gingerly at my neck where Malon had nicked me. Worse than the cut was the memory of Alok's tongue dragging along my throat and my blind trust in him. I wished I could scrub my feelings for him away with soap.

Once cleansed and dried off, I pulled on a light gray pajama set with skulls and crossbones covering the fabric.

HOLIDAY CROWN

Aunt Mel had gotten them for me last Christmas from the mortal world. It was my favorite pair.

I let down my hair, sat cross-legged on my bed, and waited in the glow of a single candle flame.

I wasn't sure if he'd come. For the past year, Alok had dreamscaped to my bedchamber whenever we came to Dahlquist. We'd stayed up talking for hours, laughing and joking. First nights were for filling one another in on what we'd been up to since the last visit. Final visits were filled with anguish and longing for our next reunion. Back then, we'd never had enough time together.

There was no longing tonight.

I doubted he'd come, anyway. Not after everything that had happened. But still I waited, heart squeezing tightly. As time slithered on, my breathing evened out, and my eyelids grew heavy. The bed beneath me beckoned for me to surrender to sleep. The candle burned low. As the flame sank farther down, a ripple of light appeared at the end of the bed. My spine stiffened as Alok's outline took shape, filling in with his features until he looked as though he was really there. He still wore the embroidered jacket, which was slightly too big for him, but it wouldn't be long before he grew into it. His black-and-blue-streaked hair appeared windblown and his eyes bright, despite their dark coloring. My heart beat erratically, anger rising in me. Today, I'd lost a lover and a friend.

I folded my arms beneath my chest. We stared at one another, saying nothing. Alok didn't move from his spot. I was the one to break the silence.

"Come to say your final goodbye?" I asked, not masking my disdain.

He drank me in with his dark eyes. I braced myself against his pull, concentrating fiercely on the mass of betrayal he'd put me through.

"I'm here to make you a promise." That voice sent shivers of unease through me. "You will be mine one day, Fraya. This I vow, and as you know, Fae don't lie."

I scoffed. "I'd worry more about your personal safety, Alok. As soon as Liri finds out about the trick you pulled, he won't rest until he's hunted you down and ended you—same as he did to your horrid father."

Alok's projection darkened. My words were cruel, but I didn't care. There was nothing romantic about Alok's promise. I heard it for what it really was. A threat. No one fucking threatened me. If he thought I'd let him off gently because of past kisses, then he was out of his mind. I needed him to understand that he was dead to me.

I unfolded my arms and sat up on my knees, glaring across the bed at Alok. "Let me make you a vow of my own. After what you did, you're the last male I'd ever give myself to. Thank Sky Mother my cousin walked in on us in time to save me from making the worst mistake of my life."

Alok's jaw tightened. "You don't mean that."

"Oh yes, I do." I laughed humorously.

HOLIDAY CROWN

Alok's fingertips skimmed his jawline as he regarded me. Despite my oath, his eyes shone glossy and bright, filled with conviction. "You'll want me again one day, Fraya. And when that day comes, I will be there for you."

I didn't get another opportunity to rebuff him. The candle guttered out, and with it, Alok disappeared in the darkened room, leaving behind his disturbing promises.

CHAPTER ELEVEN

Melarue

Flames danced from the crackling fire in the hearth of our Pinemist cottage. Lyklor and I lay naked atop a thick fuzzy rug, steadying our breaths after completing another round of passionate lovemaking. Outside our windows, snow drifted down in lazy swirls.

I could feel the glow in my cheeks. Coming here had been the best decision. We'd never enjoyed the cottage to ourselves until now. Sometimes a bit of cozy tranquility was just the thing. Plus, I'd decided I wanted our child to be conceived in the elven realm.

Lyklor propped himself up on one elbow and grinned his devilish smile. "Do you feel pregnant?"

"I feel hungry." I rubbed my tummy.

"That's a good sign," Lyklor said.

"Right," I snorted. "A sign we need to fuel up before we head back."

Lyklor's face fell. "So soon?"

I twisted my lips to one side in thought. We'd had four blissful days together, but my heart ached to be with both my mates. I missed Ryo and the boys. I missed being a family. And I felt sorta guilty about giving Ryo the slip in Dubai. If he'd left us alone, he would never know we'd snuck off someplace else. I'd find out soon enough.

I ran three fingers over my golden king's muscled chest. His warm, soft skin felt like silk against mine. If I didn't stop myself, we could end up entwined together on the rug for another week. Wouldn't be such a bad thing, but—

"We should at least check in and make sure the twins haven't terrorized anyone," I said. Being a mom came with responsibilities.

Lyklor grunted. "With the help of Aerith and Jhaeros, I'm sure Ryo has everything under control. What could possibly go wrong?"

EPILOGUE

Aerith

Christmas Eve, The Following Year

Frost crystallized against the windowpanes of our Pinemist manor home. A white wintery landscape spread out across the grounds. Inside, the rooms and halls were decked out with garlands, wreaths, giant plastic candy canes, snowflake candleholders, and even a jolly little doll dressed in red called an Elf on the Shelf. Folas had helped portal me back and forth from the mortal world to load up on holiday sale items after last Christmas.

If Mel and the kids wanted Christmas, I'd give them Christmas!

Arrangements had already been made with Hensley and Liri to cover the castle this holiday. It was my baby niece's first Christmas, and we all wanted her to spend it in Pinemist, especially after last holiday's debacle. My family and I hadn't been to Dahlquist since Alok Elmray's attempt at the crown. There had been no word of him afterward. Liri had scouts scouring the realm for Alok's whereabouts. The first place they checked was his mother's home of Frostweather, where they'd discovered Oreal had remarried a noble Fae of influence and wealth. Alok's twin, whom Malon had spoken of, was a female who lived with her mother and stepfather. At least she hadn't been planted at Ravensburg, biding her time the way Alok had. I still couldn't believe someone so young would try to take over the castle with only his weakened uncle for help. That was youth and Faerie for you. If Alok had any sense, he'd stay hidden permanently.

In addition to hunting for Alok, Liri had taken a special interest in Lark after learning his nephew had killed his uncle Malon. He'd thrown Lark an outrageously extravagant masquerade, even by Faerie standards, at the palace.

"He's going to spoil the boy," Mel had grumbled to me later.

"Like you don't," I'd countered.

Mel's eyes had bulged. "Aerith! He had a twelve-foot portrait painted of Lark holding the sword that killed Malon. It's hanging outside the throne room. He's having a stone statue made in Lark's likeness to grace the courtyard. Ugh! I can already see it going to my son's head."

"Eh," I'd said with a shrug. "I'm sure it will be a passing phase. If it lasts too long, Fraya would be happy to knock him off his high horse."

Mel, not knowing the gender of her child at the time, had expressed her wishes for a good-natured little girl like Fraya who would never cause her mother distress. My sister didn't know about Fraya and Alok. I wasn't about to mortify Fraya more than necessary. My daughter had thrown herself into her archery tournaments, becoming something of a celebrity in the elven realm. She'd moved on. Met a nice male Jhaeros and I both approved of, even if we still weren't ready for her to date. At least this male was an elf and, more importantly, not an Elmray.

Fraya sang in the sitting room, accompanying Fhaornik as he plucked the cords to "Last Christmas" on his ukulele. On my way to the kitchen, I paused inside the doorframe to watch them. Fraya wore leggings and a stylish knit sweater with little white penguins and snowmen lining the snug dark blue fabric. Our blind butler had on a bulky sweater with a reindeer wearing sunglasses. Mine was Santa riding a unicorn.

Fraya matched the song to Fhaornik's strums. The lyrics caught on my heartstrings as Fraya sang about being kissed and fooled. My daughter lifted her chest and flashed me a reassuring smile as she belted out the repeat chorus with gusto. That was Fraya, my brave, bold, beautiful daughter. She deserved sunshine and rainbows and an adoring male elf to treat her like the treasure she was.

I turned away as Fraya sang out the next set of lyrics.

The scent of baked sugar and molasses drew me to the kitchen, where Mrs. Calarel was busy mixing color into bowls of frosting on the wide counter. She looked festive in her red-and-white-striped apron. Seeing me, she smiled without stopping. Trays of tree-shaped sugar cookies covered the counters where they'd been set to cool off. Inside the cupboard, bags of candies were stacked on a shelf.

Once Mel and her brood arrived, we'd frost and decorate the cookies, followed by sledding on Market Hill, then hot cocoa back at the house. After we'd warmed up, we'd go back outside and pick out a tree from the back property to cut down and cover in ornaments inside the sitting room while Fhaornik and Fraya serenaded everyone with more holiday songs from the human world.

Yep, Mel wasn't the only one capable of going all out with the festivities. This Christmas, I was all in.

We'd attached a bell to the guest room door upstairs so we'd know when they used the portal access there. I wasn't close enough to hear them. Jhaeros came rushing into the kitchen looking so dang cute in his fuzzy Abominable Snowman sweater.

"They're here," he announced.

We reached the foyer at the same time as Mel and her family. Gleeful greetings, hugs, and kisses were exchanged. Fraya beat me to the baby. At four months, Melody was the cutest little bundle of joy. Wrapped in a soft pink blanket, Fraya hugged her baby cousin to her chest, cooing over her. I pressed a gentle kiss over Melody's soft head of light brown hair then held out my arms. Sighing, Fraya handed over my niece.

"Who is the sweetest, cutest little girl?" I rubbed my nose against Melody's.

"Ugh, Aerith, stop," Mel said, stepping over to me. "Melody is a badass."

"Who loves pink," Ryo said with a chuckle. "She cries whenever Mel tries to give her the blue or green blankie."

Mel looked skyward and groaned. "Hopefully it's just a newborn phase she'll grow out of quickly."

"I don't know, Mel. You might have a girlie girl on your hands," I said with a chuckle. I cuddled my baby niece against me. "What do you think, Melody? Will you love pink and purple, glitter and sparkles, mermaids and unicorns?"

"Shh! Don't give her ideas," Mel hissed. "They're extremely impressionable at this age." She glanced sideways at her mates, who appeared to be poking fun at Jhaeros's sweater. Lowering her voice, Mel whispered, "Don't give Lyklor or Ryo ideas either. They got way too excited in the girls' aisle of the toy store last year. Ugh."

Hmm, Mel might not like the pink "Little Princess" onesie and headband bow Jhaeros and I had gotten—one of many gifts for our new niece. Oh well. It sounded like Melody would love it, and that's what mattered.

I happened to like pink, and I was still a badass.

"Where's Dad?" Mel asked, craning her head around the foyer.

"He was invited to come over for Christmas tomorrow."

"And not a day sooner," Mel said under her breath.

Hey, my house, my rules. It wasn't like Christmas meant anything to our father, anyway. He'd just want to butt in and wrestle Melody from my arms.

HOLIDAY CROWN

"What about Folas and Gayla?" I asked. The blond guard had told me they might not come.

"They'll be here tomorrow for the day," Mel said.

My heart surged with happiness. Those two were like family, more so than my father or Shalendra. We didn't see much of my middle sister. She and her mate lived a day's travel from Pinemist and were always busy with their wine shop and the special events they organized. Jhaeros, Fraya, and I visited them from time to time.

After decorating—and sampling—cookies, everyone bundled up for the trek to Market Hill. The dads carried sleds while I held on to Melody stuffed inside a pink winter one-piece and hat with little hearts around the rim.

Fraya led our group in a song of "Jingle Bells." "'Dashing through the snow, in a one-horse open sleigh. Through the fields we go, laughing all the way.'"

Reed and Ronin really got into the following "ha, ha, has." Fraya broke off to sidle up to Lark and demand, "Why aren't you singing, Lark?"

Dressed in a dark gray peacoat, Lark lifted his regal chin. "The eldest prince of Dahlquist doesn't go around skipping and singing mortal melodies."

"Oh, I see." Fraya rolled her eyes, stopping behind him to gather snow into a ball before pelting him hard in the back.

"Hey!" Lark cried, trying to brush off the snow. Fraya had picked a hard to reach spot. I imagined she'd chosen her aim carefully.

Mel laughed gleefully, clapping her mittened hands. "Way to go, Fraya!"

"Thanks, Mom," Lark said with a huff.

Mel smirked. "Just keeping it real, dude."

"Yeah, dude," Reed chorused, puffing up his chest and strutting over the snow with exaggerated airs.

Ronin snickered. His mirth was cut off by the snowball Lark pelted him with, followed by one to Reed's head.

The twins didn't wait around for more. Balling snow in their gloved hands, they returned fire, missing Lark when he ducked out of shot. Soon it was a free-for-all between the kids until they decided to band together and go after the dads.

"Shields!" Jhaeros bellowed, raising his sled.

Ryo and Lyklor didn't have to be told twice. The inner tubes they'd carried at their sides were lifted in time to block balls of snow that broke apart on impact. The children laughed while Mel cheered them on.

Snuggling baby Melody closer, I watched my family from a safe distance with the widest grin. I wanted to bottle this moment up in a snow globe and hold on to it forever.

###

Right. Let's take a moment to address the unicorn in the room. The Royal Conquest Saga has unfinished business.

HOLIDAY CROWN

Keep reading for a special holiday message and update on what's coming next. The fun continues in the Royal Conquest Heirs series, starting with *The Golden Prince*!

AUTHOR'S NOTE

Lovely readers, winter can be a time of loneliness and holiday blues. With that in mind, I wanted to bring you some holiday cheer. You are a treasured part of this adventure, and I love sharing this escape with you.

This series may not be family friendly, but it's full of family love. With that in mind, I would like to express my love for my mortal family—in-laws, out-laws, half siblings, and all. Your loving support is more precious than all the jewels in Faerie. To my husband, Seb, this entire saga would only exist inside my imagination if not for you. To my mom and Gary, your love and generosity blows my mind.

This past summer, I lost my father, Karl. It came out of the blue; a shock for everyone. At the time, I was writing *Moon Cursed* (Wolf Hollow Shifters, book four). The news was devastating. Completing that book was a struggle when I felt emotionally depleted. I took time out to grieve. I reconnected with family. I did extra meditations, long walks, listened to music, and danced around the house belting out song lyrics (including Christmas tunes). Inspired by my dad's upbeat nature, I made a commitment to honor his memory by reclaiming my sense of humor and fun.

After turning in *Moon Cursed* to my developmental editor, I asked myself, "What's next?" The end of the novel was set up in a way that leads naturally to book five. But I was in the mood for more laugh-out-loud outlandish fun. Back when I was completing *Three Kings*, I made notes for a possible Royal Conquest Christmas novella. Chances felt fifty-fifty as to whether I would take time out to write it. At the beginning of September, I decided I'd give myself one day to determine whether I should continue. Oh, holly berries! Laughter erupted from my lips as my fingers clacked over the keyboard. My face ached from grinning. I knew before lunchtime that there was no turning back.

Thank you to Team Queen. My editors: Kelly Hashway (I love how much you love Ryo and look out for him); Hollie Westring (you're always full of good cheer, no matter what time of year); and Roxanne Willis (meeting you in person this past September was an absolute highlight moment of my year). To my reading queens and kings, you all are my unicorns and rainbows spreading magic and light. An extra special thank you to the following readers, who brainstormed baby names with me (boys and girls to keep it a surprise—heh, heh): Irina Wolpers, Kelly Stepp, Leah Ann Storm, Hanife Ormerod, Tiffany Loyd, Kristen Smith, Pam Foster . . . and to the ladies who came up with "Melody"—a pink, sparkly "thank you" to Sandra Richardson and Crystal R. Stacey! I know that makes for two Mels, but the moment I saw the name, it felt perfect for the newest addition to the Elmray family and festive for a holiday baby.

And now, dear reader, this is where I might have wished you a happy holiday, but holidays aren't always happy, and

HOLIDAY CROWN

I'm trying to avoid clichés. Instead, allow me to send warm wishes your way and invite you to find the humor, the silly, the little something special that sneaks into your day, and to have a laugh wherever you can find one.

Since I'm clearly having trouble letting go of these characters, I will see you in the *Royal Conquest Heirs* follow-up novellas, starting with *The Golden Prince* (Lark), then *The Dark Pretender* (Alok).

For more interactions, updates, and fantastical musings, I invite you to join my reading group on Facebook at The Fantasy Fix with Nikki Jefford. Let's have fun!

Nikki Jefford
September 2019

NIKKI NEWS!

Sign up for Nikki's spam-free newsletter. Receive cover reveals, excerpts, and new release news before the general public; enter to win prizes; and get the scoop on special offers, contests, and more.

Visit Nikki's website to put your name on the list. Make sure to confirm your email so you won't miss out:

nikkijefford.com

See you on the other side!

MORE PLACES TO FIND NIKKI JEFFORD

Instagram:

www.instagram.com/nikkijefford

Facebook:

www.facebook.com/authornikkijefford

Twitter:

@NikkiJefford

BookBub:

www.bookbub.com/profile/nikki-jefford

GoodReads:

www.goodreads.com/author/show/5424286.Nikki_Jefford

SLAYING, MAGIC MAKING, RUNNING WILD, AND RULING THE WORLD!

Discover your next fantasy fix with these riveting paranormal romance and fantasy titles by Nikki Jefford:

AURORA SKY: VAMPIRE HUNTER

Night Stalker
Aurora Sky: Vampire Hunter
Northern Bites
Stakeout
Evil Red
Bad Blood
Hunting Season
Night of the Living Dante
Whiteout
True North

SPELLBOUND TRILOGY

Entangled
Duplicity
Enchantment
Holiday Magic

WOLF HOLLOW SHIFTERS

Wolf Hollow
Mating Games
Born Wild
Moon Cursed

ROYAL CONQUEST SAGA

Stolen Princess
False Queen
Three Kings
Holiday Crown
The Golden Prince
The Dark Pretender

ABOUT THE AUTHOR

Nikki Jefford is a third-generation Alaskan now living in the Pacific Northwest with her French husband and their Westie, Cosmo. When she's not reading or writing, she enjoys nature, hiking, and motorcycling. Nikki is the author of the *Royal Conquest Saga*, *Wolf Hollow Shifters* series, *Aurora Sky: Vampire Hunter* series, and *Spellbound Trilogy*.

Made in the USA
Coppell, TX
08 November 2022